D1258516

Love and Will

Other Books by Stephen Dixon

No Relief
Work
Too Late
Quite Contrary
14 Stories
Movies
Time to Go
Fall & Rise
Garbage
The Play

LOVE
AND
WILL
=
TWENTY
STORIES
BY
STEPHEN
DIXON

A PARIS REVIEW EDITION
BRITISH AMERICAN PUBLISHING

MIDDLEBURY COLLEGE LIBRARY

Many of these short stories were published, in somewhat different form, in the following periodicals: *Ambit* (London), *American Review, Boundary 2, Chicago Review, Chouteau Review, Croton Review, Harper's, The Literary Review, Michigan Quarterly Review, New Departures in Fiction, North American Review, The Paris Review, Poet & Critic, Quarterly West, Seneca Review, South Carolina Review, Story Quarterly, Telescope, Transatlantic Review, Triquarterly, 2Plus2*

These stories are works of fiction. Names, characters, places and incidents either are the product of the author's imagination or are used fictitiously. Any resemblance to actual events or locales or persons, living or dead, is entirely coincidental.

Copy © 1989 by Stephen Dixon
All rights reserved, including the right of reproduction in whole or in part in any form.
Published by British American Publishing/Paris Review Editions
3 Cornell Road, Latham, NY 12110
Manufactured in the United States of America
93 92 91 90 89 5 4 3 2 1

Library of Congress Cataloging-in-Publication Data
Dixon, Stephen, 1936—
    Love and will
      p.   cm.
    ISBN 0–945167–20–2 : $17.95

Contents

To Anne, Sophia and Antonia

Love and Will

Say about an hour ago she said well I don't want to beat around the bush, Will, I'm deeply in love with this man. She wasn't being cruel or rude. What was she being? Of course not cruel or rude. It's starting to snow. When I was in her apartment just before, she said when you were outside did it seem as though it might snow? I said why, does she want to go out? She said she just wants to know, that's all. I told her I was never in my life able to tell. But truthful is what I suppose she was. I don't know. But certainly truthful is what she came closest to being to me at the time. I don't know anything right now except right now I'd like nothing better than to be on top or underneath or at the side or moving at intervals all around her but inside her and with our tongues tied and playful and bodies tight. But there she was. After a while rather tired of me and wanting me to go. Though looking so calm at first. Kissing me when I entered the apartment though now instead of a whole mouth I got the tip of her lips. The peck. And stepping back from me when I put out my arms to hug. And when I finally got her into my hug, placing her arms around me weakly and patting my back as if to console me for my loss. Then holding my hands mother to child. Speaking to me man to man. Looking so sorrowfully at me as if for the pain she was causing me which

1

she couldn't help me get out of or over or undo. It's done. She's in love.

Listen, she said, trite, ridiculous or whatever this might sound to you, I'm in love with my entire being. So am I, I said. She said she doesn't believe me. I said did I say it was with you? Anyway what you say doesn't sound ridiculous or anything else to me because I too strongly believe in love. That's good, she said. Or believe strongly in love—they both sound right. That's good, she said. Or I just believe in love, I said, why should I refer to strength? But me she could easily dispose of. The lesser of two loves. Rather the one she said she was growing to love. Or at least could have grown to love. Or whatever it was she said about love. But what she did say was that for a while she felt she might have liked to learn to live with me but could now only afford from a distance to like. The one she loved deeply was the other who she'll be flying to during her Easter break in two weeks. In London where she said he says he has a large and lovely Victorianlike flat. Saying things to me like that. And that she's so sorry it had to come to this. Her oneway bliss. Because she was really quite content with me till she met this new man. It was all such a fluke. A girlfriend called her up. She said she knew this English fellow about to leave for England whom she wanted her to meet before he went. He came over for tea for an hour and stayed with her for a week before he took his flight last night. For a few days during this time she kept telling me on the phone she's sick and very tired and thinks she's coming down with the flu. Tonight she said she was fairly sick and tired but seems to have escaped the flu.

She also told me she thinks I'm a bit off. That she didn't want to say it. That she in fact at first didn't believe it. She said she thought when I said certain things she didn't understand that she was being obtuse. Now she's certain that many things I say are a bit off. I said off? She said off. I said excuse me but off to where? To China? To the provinces? Off to the outer regions of our solar plexus or the inner legions of hell? She said off like that. No not like that. Now I was being belligerent, defensive, reactive, if maybe a little off. What she's talking about off is when I say things she thinks I think come to me from faraway places or just pop presto magically in my head and which she said I repeat with total confidence without really knowing what I said. Because aren't people obliged to understand what they're saying to other people aloud? she said. What they say to themselves or too low for anyone to hear is another story—she supposes anything goes there. I said I suppose so unless what the person's saying to someone is said more for the poetry of the words—the sounds. She said these off things she thinks I say don't sound poetical or anything else to her except off. I said I didn't say they did. And that she's right. I often say off things simply because I think they might or do sound metaphysically comical or epistemologically profound or just plain bright or yuk yuk funny and she'll enjoy my company more for my having said them than if I hadn't or some such stuff. Then you agree? she said. I said cross my hope and heart to die. She said that's the first time we agreed on anything since that first time we ever agreed on anything which was when we agreed that her sister's Great Dane puppies we were watching suckling their mama were performing a very sensual act. I told her we didn't even initially agree on that. That I didn't think the puppies were doing anything especially sensual in their suckling till later that night when I dreamt of those suckling puppies and in my dream became one of those puppies nuzzling my face between the back legs to get at the two hindmost nipples and that instead of suckling a nipple it was like being with my tongue and lips down in there doing it to a woman which I did to her when we woke. She said she doesn't remember that. I said I'm sorry but it was only as a result of my dream and between the time of our waking up and making love that I agreed with her that those suckling puppies had performed a sensual act.

It's snowing harder. Where oh where in my pocket is my collapsible green felt emergency harsh weather hat? I'm walking to my parents' apartment of thirty-three years. People scurry past all four ways. Ahead a block away a figure slips and trips before he can get himself upright to flip over again. I pull down my hat tightly so it won't blow off. If Dana were with me now she might walk right behind me holding my waist and then say she sees she can't be protected from the snow and cold this way and can we take a cab? If I said let's walk a little more, as I like a strong wind with lots of curlicuing large flakes, she'd probably say she'll pay. It's eleven blocks south along Central Park West from her building and then a right turn down a sidestreet to a brownstone halfway down. I pass the statue I passed with Dana a few weeks ago when I said remember the time I told you I once saw one of the museum's custodians polishing the bronze testes of Theodore Roosevelt's horse? She said then that as she said before she thinks the experience has to be experienced to be appreciated though not visualized. Tonight she said her scalp had mercifully stopped itching during the time David was with her though resumed a few minutes after I came in. I said I suppose that's reason enough for falling deeply in love with him, seeing how she's compared her up till then irremediable fungus to thousands of microscopic devils trying to claw their way out of each of her hair follicles and then getting lost in her hair, but why doesn't she come right out with it and say she thinks I'm the main cause of her itchy scalp? She said she thought she just did. No she only looked at me teasingly as if to say she thought she just did.

I'm sure my mother's asleep. She usually reads in her room while sipping from a half glass of sweet wine for a half hour after she puts my father to bed at nine. He'll be asleep in his hospital bed in the living room, the room closest to the kitchen and bathroom, where during the colder months he spends most of his waking day. He'll be facing the window. The floor-length curtains inches away from him will be fastened together by safety pins. I'll turn him over as I do every night I sleep home. About once a month I must rush him in his wheelchair to the bathroom so he can make two. He can't turn over by himself. We've been warned he can get bed sores if he isn't turned at least once a night and that in the morning his muscles and bones on one side will most likely ache. And he can develop red spots on his ankles from the pressure of one foot lying too long on the other and his having dislodged the pillow placed between his feet. And because he's a diabetic the red spots can lead to open wounds which can lead to a foot being cut off. Before I turn him over I'll say urinate first. I'll place the urinal between his thighs and stick his penis inside if he's too tired to do so or can't locate it. I'll hear the splash against the plastic and then say through now? and he'll say no or yes. If it's no I'll take the urinal away a minute later and empty and wash it out. Then I'll turn him over and place the pillow between his feet. Two Chux between his penis and thighs in case he has an accident overnight. Cover him up with the top sheet folded a few inches over the blankets and place the urinal beside the Gelusils and bell on the table-tray beside his bed. I'll say comfortable? and he'll say yes. I'll kiss him on the forehead and say goodnight. Maybe touch his cheek or run my hand across his face or pat his shoulder or head and shut out all the lights and say sleep well and he might murmur thanks. I'll close the louver doors to the kitchen. Get a glass of wine from the refrigerator and read in bed with another glass of wine. Maybe return to the kitchen for a third or fourth or fifth glass of wine before I feel sleepy enough for sleep.

Tonight she said that's your problem when I said I'm sure if I had showed her more affection and attention this past month she never would have become interested in this English guy. She had placed on the table a plate of different French cheeses she had picked up at the same store she bought the closest American bread to a baguette. I said I'll get a knife. She said break it with your hands. I said it isn't easy breaking butter with your hands unless the cubes are frozen solid and it also gets very messy smearing it on bread with your fingertips. She said she'll get it but I said stay. I got up so I could get behind her. Her back was to the kitchen. I leaned over her from behind with the knife in my hand and kissed her lips. She let us linger there but when I tried opening her mouth it wouldn't budge. Maybe you better go, she said. I spoke about passion. I forget whose. Maybe hers, mine, ours. She said must you yell? I was putting my shoes on at the time. I said when I speak about passion I sometimes have to do it passionately. And passion to me is the essential, Yeats said, I said. I told her that was in a letter he dictated or wrote. I know because I read it yesterday. And I know I read it yesterday, I said, because if I had read it the day before yesterday I wouldn't have remembered the quote and if I read it today I would have remembered if the letter had been dictated or written. She said someone else once said. I said Shakespeare always said. She said Shakespeare isn't the one she's thinking of although one of his characters did say give me that man that is not passion's slave, which she thinks applies to her here. My shoes, coat and muffler were now on. She said she forgets which play it's from though it was in one of the textbooks she taught from last term, but let's call it a night, Will, she said. I said I can't and I'm not going to transform into the little boy she says I sometimes become when I don't get what I want. Hamlet, she said. Act scene, seen act, I should have said. But I said my stomach hurts and I'm feeling awful and I don't want to be alone tonight. She said well what do I expect her to do? I said her sleeping with me now would be a very considerate thing to do. She said not tonight. But you don't even know, I said. Didn't one time in bed you didn't want to do it when I did and I stirred you up into wanting to and later you said you were glad I hadn't let you fall asleep straight off? She said she'll call me at the end of the week and we'll meet. I quickly calculated. Today's Monday. Four days. Too long. Maybe the end of the week meant Sunday to her. I said we can simply sleep beside one another if she likes, arm around arm, not even that if she doesn't like. Just in the same bed if she likes. Or if she likes I'll place a board between us if she has a board or a column of thumbtacks down the middle of the bed if she prefers. I said do you have any tacks? She said no. I said what if I just sleep on the living room couch surrounded by thumbtacks and broken glass and you in your own bed in your room? No that won't do, I said. What have I come to? I said. What about the time she was so warm to me when I was sick? It started in a movie house. We had to leave before the picture was over but she said she didn't mind in the least. Not if I was sick. She gave me medicine, a back rub. I had fever and chills. She tucked me in, made me mint tea. Paid for the cab. Untucked me, got in beside me. No clothes on. Oh what a sight. I wore her shirt. She turned down the electric blanket. Warmed me with what she for the first time out of many called her hot box body. And next morning I was well. The infamous ten-and-a-half hour virus had passed. Doctor Dana I said when she gave me tomato juice in bed. Just old Doc Dan to my friends she said when she took the glass. I don't know if it was when she took the glass. I do know it was tomato. I think she that night stirred me up to doing what I originally didn't feel like though I'm now not so sure. I think I said you'll get sick. I think she said don't fret about me. Did we come? Was it fun? Tonight I said passionately that I won't speak about passion passionately anymore tonight or even dispassionately or even the word passion or passionate or passionately or passional or even passionless or -ateness or passion fruit or flower or week or -tide or play or Sunday or even pass in or passing or pass sing or passengers sing or passenger pigeons used to sing or any words like that. None. I promise. Heart my cross and die to hope. I'll be passionless. No words even near to passion. Not even passive, passage, passport, Passaic, passe partout or even passe or partout.

By now I was at the door. At the door I said I'll stay a while longer if she still wants to talk. I'd like to talk. Stay then, she said, but please not for long. So I again thought there was still some hope. What I wanted most was to get us both into bed. But that I already said. But that I still want to do. Just to get this horrid night through. Because tomorrow, she said, I think tomorrow we both have to go to work. But how am I going to get through work? Should I call in sick and lose a per diem day's pay? She gets paid when she phones in ill. She teaches at college, I'm at junior high. She works one third of my hours and gets twice as much pay. Her work's more than not intellectually stimulating and emotionally satisfying while I come home physically exhausted and emotionally and mentally drained every workday. But she takes the subway to work while I walk the three blocks to school and run home for lunch. I shut the door. Close call I think I thought then. And sit at her table without ever again removing my muffler, coat or gloves. In the movies we used to hold hands. Tonight I said I bet in a month this piggy finger of hers will have rings. In the street it was arms around waists and also hands. And one night at Ray's place she fell asleep with her head in my lap. I petted and played with it as I would with a cat. Lights were out, logs were on. Later she said she didn't much care for my friend and his girl but liked their fire. She also had this bad habit of bugging taxi men. You're taking us too far out of our way she used to say. Shhh, I told her, better gypped than dead. She said in the cab I looked quite strong but wasn't that brave. But then another time she spoke about my courage but said I lacked common sense. And then a third time she feared how physically weak I sometimes appeared and that—

"Beep beep yourself. I said beep beep it up your nose. I said the pedestrian's got the right of way. Especially in a snow and sleet storm and even if the red light's against him which it wasn't. Oh don't give me that hand over the ear you can't hear. Go on, go on, before you miss your precious light. Then open your window a tinkle if you want to understand." There they go. Waving goodbye to me as if departing for across the States. Bye-bye now mama and papa and all the relatives, afraid for a little chill. Your door's open I should have yelled. Your back lights aren't working, muffler's hanging, fender's dragging, tire's flat or very short of air. I'm sure they thought he's a crack. Nut job to say the least. Looks so dopey in his nitwit Pinocchio hat. La la—listen to your tape deck and stereo set. Turn up the heater some more you Cadillac people, cushy as you are in your own mushy homes. But what do I know what kind of people they are? Besides it was a Buick. Be by me now, sweet, and I wouldn't rage at all. Die my heart and cross to hope. I'd laugh. Ya ya. Out loud. Ha ha. We'd nip from my mouthwash flask of gay sherry.

Four days ago Thursday I like an idiot called. How's your flu faring along? Health and energy sufficiently restored to have dinner tomorrow night, tonight? Clown, fool, greenhorn, tool. French or fish at Oscar's Salt of the Sea I was about to say. She said this iniquitous illness and inexplicable exhaustion and she'll call me in a few days. I came over anyway. Rang her bell. First a how do you do to her doorman who doubles at suddenly starting and short-stopping her elevator up. Five, but he says he knows. Flowers under my arm. Brush breath sweet, dentin and cementum dehypersensitized. I wanted a yes or no or whether in her indispositions she was giving me the ole heave ho. I also had the collected shorter works of Wordsworth she once wanted to reread. David? No, Will. Just a minute and in a minute she opened the door. Clothed only in a body hose from the belly-button down. Didn't think you'd come. Putting a top on she said she doesn't want David finding her naked with another man. David's the English fellow she's been wanting to tell me about who's staying with her this week. She asked what I'm doing and I said looking for his luggage to throw into the backyard. I threw her the flowers instead. For David, I said. She laughed. I started for the door. But why'd she laugh? Wordworth I must have let just slide down my leg to the floor. The meaning of my flowers-for-David remark was unknown to me then but could now be made to seem clear. Garlands for the victor? To the swines goes the spoiled. Pearls before oxen. Rich gifts wax poor when givers prove unkind. I don't know. Truer sayings have been said but none as known—no. Say it with flowers. All work and no play makes Will a dull boy. She wants to explain things about David and herself but I'm already two flights down the service stairs. Don't ever try to contact me again is what I yelled.

I called her tonight and she said sure if you want to come by. She didn't know how it had happened with David so fast—would I like a beer? She's grown addicted to Heineken's this past week. A girlfriend rang her up. But I've been over all that. Maybe I'll ring her when I get home. Hello, London calling. Oooh our mouths. Our attacking genitals. I liked us best when—no. The one post she lost her mental self in most was—no. In the Brooklyn Botanical Gardens last month—no. Same day we watched the bonsai grow and she zipped us through the Van Gogh exhibit, afraid I might faint from the crowds. Ballet, dinner parties, never a stage play or sporting event, long park walks, and when it was nipping cold, backwards short runs. Do you also dance to records and thumping FM while you're both undressed? and she said yes. Next thing you'll say is he's as loving and rutty as I when you're both entangled and compressed and she said she's afraid even more so yes. I told her I never quite felt I was good enough for her anyway and she said she was surprised she got to like me as much as she did. My moral code and standards were usually too rigid and high, too many times she felt compelled to concur with me or be browbeaten, there was something disquietingly revealing about the fact that I never got along with any of her male or female friends. Before we met, she never before told me, she vowed never again to date a psychologist or any man too analytical of himself or critical of her. No, David's a psychologist, though she thinks they're called another name in England as lawyers and lorries are, and maybe too self-analytical though not at all critical and like her a bit weary of the supersensitive and inordinately cautious and just plain brilliant and creative types and loves lots of dumb horsing around. Baby powder's what she used to put on in the morning if we made love the evening or hour before and she was late for work. What could her fellow subway riders and her students be thinking, she said, when she sits down and up comes clouds of scented smoke. Besides everything else I was too caliginous and morose. Can't stand that in a man. I can't stand it in myself so we also agreed on that. And also how good we were feeling those days when we were so often laid so well. And that the bed was our preferred mediating place in case anything between us went awry. And that there was nothing wrong with a lifelong streak of vanity, that this summer we'd try two months of northern Maine sanity, that philosophers are not doctors of philosophy who teach and lovers are not people who preach and Blake's binding with briars my joys and desires the most novel last line we knew in a non-twentieth-century poem. I'm home.

"Will?"

Let me at least remove my guaranteed waterproof shoes, my sopping socks. Why'd I throw away the guarantee? Why do I usually speedily discard vouchers, contracts, receipts, invitations, instructions, stubs, phone numbers, directions, warranties and guarantees and whatever else relevant to me in this category and rely on my time-attested incompetent memory or good luck or the buyer or seller's good faith or will?

"Junior?"

Why don't I keep a record of the checks I make out? The poems, drawings and picture-poems I send out? Where they are, how long, and if they've ever been there, how much money I've still in my account or owe or am owed and who the owers are?

"Will?"

"Coming." Why won't I wear a watch? Why do I avoid health checkups yet see my dentist twice a year? Is it only money that keeps me from buying a reliable pair of waterproof shoes or shoelike insulated boots? How come I've never been able to resist chocolate, have always hated the flavor of coffee, can't pass a day without munching several carrots, have never wanted to smoke? Why have the girls and women I've fallen in love with dumped me in a maximum of three months? Why have I always reacted to these one-sided falling aways or breakups in the same hurt sorrowful mawkish way? Why am I always so much of the same? Why are things so permanent? Why can't I tease instead of torment myself for my seemingly eternal limitations? Why can't I take my satisfactions in just the barely perceptible change? Why have I been so consistently contradictory and thus contradictorily consistent? Why is it such a struggle to lift a toilet seat when I pee when by nature I'm so unlazy? Why do I usually get nauseated in art museums and libraries and end up making runny movements in their johns? Why have I always been a whiz at mathematics and picking up languages and a dunce at any subject scientific or doing anything with a typewriter except two-finger typing and clogging the keys with eraser flecks? Is it the stars, God, gods, my hormones—

"Junior?"

—genetic code, parents, theirs, our great and grand great-grandparents and what we and all the plant and animal life we've come in contact with have breathed or ingested or something or ings or body or bodies else? Other influences influencing these influences with still even more influent influences which some people have or might have spoken or written about but which I generally find too tedious to listen to or want to learn about or have simply forgotten about and which in fact might be too complex or mazy or lost in space, time or imagination for any man in this or any of the past thousand centuries to know about if any of those or these are or is the reason or reasons I am the way I am or am what I was or am what I will probably always be?

"Will, please."

"Got you, Dad. The bows and knots in my shoelaces got shrunken tight. And I've got to get rid of these drenched socks and turn on the kitchen lights first. It's snowing outside."

"Well, come on."

"Take it easy. You've got to hold on at times too."

"Oh go take the gaspipe."

"What? Just screw yourself."

"And you take the gaspipe."

"And you go screw yourself."

I leave him holding the filled urinal. In the kitchen I open an ale. He must have used it when he heard my keys in the locks or while I was untangling my shoelaces' knots. But I don't want to be teaching lessons tonight. With his arms reared high and jug in hand he looked like a proffering trodden servant-slave in a hieroglyph. Nor if possible to Dana tomorrow about her unattractive brusqueness with cabbies and waiters or even where her fondling and positioning with me had been remiss. Some days while walking it to the john I thought I might suicidally take a swig of his piss. And morning he'll badger Mom about my conduct and she being what she is will take the brunt. She'll say I know he can be rough on you at times but he's a sick helpless man who if we want to help we've got to give in.

"Finished?"

"Yeah."

I turn him over, empty, wash out and replace the urinal on the table-tray. When he said go take the gaspipe I should have clutched my throat, gagged, fallen to the floor and played dead for a few seconds as if one of his curses had finally worked. I cover him, kiss his forehead, pat his back. "Goodnight." From what I've seen and my mother's said and said his mother's said, he's always been the same too.

"You drink too much."

"I should have left the glass inside."

"Not the glass, your breath. From alcohol. It stinks."

"Anyway it's only ale."

"Ale now, what before? Some more later. For ten years at least. From what I can imagine, longer. Your liver."

"My liver's okay. Though maybe it's not. What do I know? That a man starts off at the place where he's born and ends at the place where he dies. Sound bright? It's what the priest or anti-priest said in a movie on television I recently saw. But I should get it checked out. By an expert on foie gras. I'm the goose, take a gander. No, but maybe a bad report will give me a good scare. Though I do like to drink. But only wine with my evening mess, beer with my friends more or less, ale for what ails me, never cider cept on salads, hardly the hard stuff anymore, but you used to drink."

"I got smart. Be like me."

"Why should I be like you?"

"Because you're not as smart."

"Well, by the time you wake up tomorrow I'll try to have become as smart as you."

"Not a chance."

"Why so sure?"

"I'm tired."

"Ah the good are, when we get down to the nitty-gritty, beyond all the flim-flamming hunky-dories and icy-nicies to the heeby-jeeby really trulies, is that you only tolerate me as much as you do because you think I might beat it out of here and leave you both stranded or stay and start selecting the insulin needles I inject you with daily for their barbs."

"Go to sleep. I'm tired."

"Pleasant dreams."

"The pills?"

"They're here. Two of them, one for each stomach. Tissues in your pajama pocket. Urinal within easy reach. Bell. Chux. I forgot. Your teeth?"

"Your mom."

I place the Chux between his penis and thighs. "Now you're set. Sleep well."

"Thanks."

I kiss his forehead and shut the light. In the kitchen I open another ale and dial Dana's number.

"Hello," she says.

"Hello, London calling."

"Yes?"

"Sorry there, Miss. Can't hear you my very best. Must be a bad connect. Transatlantic tubes must have become untied or innerpacific allied." But I can just as well imagine our conversation and I hang up. She'd say Will? I'd say the tubes are retied now, Miss. Called in London's leading gynecologist for the job, pronouncing gyn as gin. She'd say aren't they called cables instead of tubes and I'd say fables instead of cables and maybe then hang up. Maybe she'll call back. Twice before when I hung up she did and both times I said we'd been disconnected and we talked about the continually declining phone service in New York till she said didn't we discuss this same subject last time we were cut off? My continually declining glass. Star fright, snow blight, I wish tonight for tomorrow an empty class. Maybe stout rather than ale or sour mash straight up or with water and or ice. Perhaps a sketch of her in bed on her back in her bedroom on the back of an ordinary white postcard will suffice. Or a story drawn in two strips of four boxes apiece on a postcard showing scenes of my life serially from the start of a standard weekday. Jiggling alarm off at eight, pastry shop clock on my way to work late, teachers' punch-in clock, wall classroom clocks accompanied by students' mocks and socks and then three o'clock schlock and clock store clocks on the block and maybe Dana's shock and my father's pocket tick-tock and again me in bed behind locks beside my Baby Ben clock drinking bock from a flock of crocks. Or a long amusing letter. Sent several and she said there's almost nothing about you I like better. I'll write I'm leaving the city forever as I can't endure being in it without her. Kissing the folks adios on the avenue I stick out my thumb. Plans are after I get out of the city to make it cross country on the bum. Hop in, a shopper holding open a shopping bag will say. Hop aboard, a boy on a skateboard will say. Hop off, says the bus driver when I can't cough up the exact fare. Hop to it, says the motorcyclist after slicing off my thumbing thumb with a razor blade and breezing away with it leaving my thumb base bare. I swaddle the hand in a rag, flag down a cab, say tail that motorcyclist who's copped my thumb, as I read if you've lopped off a digit you've no more than an hour to get it sewn back on. I find the thumb on a manhole, rush with it to a hospital, the receptionist sends me to the toe-finger section, I get lost in the many corridors and wind up in the room for cadaver dissections, at the hospital pharmacy I ask for digitalis, for I also read doctors adhere fingers back to hands with it along with a dash of Vitalis, the pharmacist asks for my prescription slip, I say are you kidding and bleep bleep your blip blip, she says no prescription no digitalis, but no female pharmacist could be that callous, so I show her my severed thumb, as I figured she faints and lies numb, I leap over the pharmacy counter, just reprisal might be for me to savagely mount her, but I'm losing time all the time so I look for shelf D, find the digitalis and help myself to some Vitalis on shelf V, blend the two ingredients together with pestle and mortar, as the directions suggest add three tablespoons of tepid water, guzzle down the entire mixture, press thumb to hand till it again becomes a fixture, but maybe another letter or continuance of this one where in the digitalis section I also find shrinking powder, though because it's on the D shelf it's here called drinking powder, which makes me so small I can sit up in Dana's hand, after having tumbled out of the same envelope I sent her this letter in from a foreign land. But instead on the bottom of a postcard I draw my face frontwards from chin dimple to dome, and inside the word balloon above me write in wee letters the following poem. Skin of stone, rock for a heart, dead glaze and gaze for a look that once leaked longing, loving, sapless tree about to fall, cold dusty remains of burnt charcoal, bones found in a hundred-year-old grave, thousand-year-old grave, ancient Mesopotamian tomb, empty hospital room, pencil lead, desert of dead, polished ball of solid steel, endless wheel, nothing but space in a carapace, sealed airless Plexiglas box, doors opening on doors and each with numerous locks, vacuum, exosphere, or whichever atmosphere where there's no breathable air, light bulb with broken filament, lightninglike cracks in buckets of hardened cement, wall of unshatterable glass I exhaust myself trying to smash, moldy lace, unalterable obdurate face, stiff plastic, what was once elastic, but didn't I, hint I, that just seeing a woman steadily for a month is for me a torrid love affair?

I address the card to Dana, drop it in the street's mail container, dogfight, lamppost light, make everything turn out all right.

And then that Will who became Guil who wrote si jamais revient cette femme, Je lui dirais Je suit lui content.

My old man's snoring, the snow's now pouring.

Will's tight, his poems trite, maybe sleep will shorten his half-wit's height.

To her living room ceiling's attached a double-sized hammock, first time I met her she wore gobs of blue eye shadow but no other makeup.

Losing sight, nighty-night—oh one other thing she said was will you go fly a kite.

Falling, stalling.

Dog Days

I was crossing Broadway in the eighties when the light turned red and traffic sped past. I waited at the crosswalk on one of those islands in the middle of the avenue when a dog rushed at me from the benches and sunk its teeth into my leg. I tried shaking it off. It growled but wouldn't let go. I swatted its head with my book and it snapped at my swinging hand and then put its teeth back into my calf. I yelled "Goddamnit, whose dog is this, call it off."

Three transvestites were sitting on the row of benches with two more normally dressed homosexuals. They were all looking and laughing. I kicked the dog with my other foot and it yelped but ran away this time as I fell to the ground. The five men laughed much harder, seeing me on my behind. I got up. The light turned green. My pants were ripped where the dog had bit me and I felt saliva or blood or both leaking into my socks from the wound. The dog was sitting between two transvestites, licking himself. One of the transvestites tied a tattered cord to the scarf around the dog's neck and patted its head where I'd hit it. I limped over.

"That your dog?" I said.

"I'm not talking."

"You just talked, Jersey," one of the more normally dressed homosexuals said.

"Why you going and tell this nice man what my name is, you pimp and a half?"

"I didn't tell him. I was only addressing you by what I thought was your name. It isn't?"

"Why didn't you call your dog off?" I said to Jersey.

"That's my business and when I want it to be yours, I'll tell you."

"But he bit me."

"I thought he just psyched you out."

"He sunk his teeth into my leg twice."

"Oh yeah? Show me. I got to have proof."

I pulled up my pants leg to the calf. Blood was dribbling out of both sets of bites.

"Whoo whoo," one of the other transvestites said. "Show us some more leg, honey. You're getting me hot."

"Oh God," and I let my pants leg down.

"God had nothing to do with it," he said.

"Who said that before you just said it?" Jersey asked him. "Some famous old movie queen."

"Beulah."

"That's it—the grape. Oh; she was so funny and great."

"Your dog been vaccinated?" I said to Jersey.

"People are vaccinated. And for smallpox and polio, not animal bites."

"Then dog shots. Has he had them?"

"Hundreds of times."

"Where's his license?"

He looked at his nails, buffed them on his thigh. "I don't like this color," he said to the transvestite next to him. "You?"

"How do I know he hasn't rabies then?" I said.

"How do I know you haven't rabies?" Jersey said.

"Don't you think it's important I know? Be reasonable. If he has rabies, all I have to do is get treated for it."

"Now listen you. Either give us some more gam or make tracks. You're becoming a nuisance."

"He has nice legs though," the transvestite next to him said.

"Too fat," the third one said.

"Those are muscles, not fat."

The other two men were laughing behind a newspaper. Jersey was opening a bottle of nail polish. I said "You're all nuts and I'm calling a cop," and crossed the avenue.

"Bye, toots," a couple of them said. I turned around. The two other transvestites were standing and waving handkerchiefs at me. Jersey was polishing his nails.

A block away I saw two policemen talking to a man. The man was gesturing with his hands in a way I'd never seen before and when I came over, speaking a language I'd never heard.

"Excuse me, officers, but I have to report something."

"Just a second," one of them said. "This guy's trying to tell us something that's obviously pretty important to him but we can't make out a word he says. That's not some Caribbean form of Spanish or South America, is it?"

"Habla Espanol or Portuguese?" I said to the man.

"Caper hyper yoicher," he said.

"Die Deutsch. Sprechen sie Deutsch or Francais?"

"Yoicher caper hyper."

"We are trying to find out what language you are speaking or you can understand," the policeman said very slowly to him.

"Hyper yoicher caper," he seemed to say, "caper yoicher hyper."

Then he shook his head and rolled up his trouser leg and pulled down his sock and pointed to a set of teeth marks on his ankle and dried blood around it and made barking sounds and imitated an animal or human being baring his teeth and biting down hard with them.

"You've been bitten?" the policeman said.

"That's what happened to me just now," I said. "By a dog."

"It did?—Dog? Chien? Cane?" he said to the man. "Mange cane?"

"Yoicher hyper caper yoicher," the man said. "Yoicher. Yoicher."

I showed the man my own bite marks and pointed to his ankle and he nodded and smiled and said "Ya ya ya ya."

"Where?" I pointed to our bites and then to the island a block away and made barking sounds and said "There?"

"Ya ya ya ya. Caper caper hyper yoicher."

"You've both been bitten by dogs then," the policeman said. "You think the same one?"

"I think we ought to go and find out," I said.

"What do you say, Kip?" he said to his partner.

"Let's go over and see," Kip said.

We all went over to the island. The five men were still sitting there. "Officer," Jersey said, standing up as we approached them, "I want to make a complaint against this man," looking at me.

"Just a second," the policeman said. "These two men have a complaint against you. This your dog?"

"That's exactly what my complaint's about. The foreigner I've never seen till before. All I know is I'm sitting here when suddenly he's yelling and babbling at us and then left. But this one," pointing to me, "tried to accost me last night along the park side of Central Park West. When I refused to go into the park with him or do what he wanted me to right there against the park wall for the whole city to see, he said he'd come back to get his revenge on me. Well he didn't last night. But ten minutes ago he tried to attack me on this bench. That's why my dog bit him. Out of protection for me."

"That true?" Kip said to me.

"It's so ridiculous I won't even answer it," I said.

"See?" Jersey said. "Now if you don't mind, I'm exhausted and going home." He started to walk away with his dog. Kip stopped him and told him to sit.

"Why? This man only proved who's right."

Milos, the foreigner, started to shake his fist at Jersey. Jersey told him to stick it up. He shook both fists at Jersey. Jersey said "Maricon!" and turned around and shook his behind in Milos's direction. Milos jumped at him and had to be pulled away by the policemen. He shouted at Jersey "Hyper hyper yoicher caper. Caper!"

"What language he speaking?" Jersey said.

"We're trying to find out," Kip said. "Any of your friends maybe?"

"Foreign language," one of the transvestites said, sewing a button to his shirt. "I hate them. They should all be sent back on the boats tonight."

"Has your dog a license?" the policeman said to Jersey.

"What's your name, officer?" Jersey said.

"John."

"My dog has a license, John, but it must have fallen off in the scuffle with this man," meaning me.

"There was no scuffle," I said to John.

"You've already proven yourself a liar," Jersey said. "Now you should shut up."

Just then a derelict walked over and asked me what was wrong. "Dispute," I said.

"Got a quarter?" he said.

"Will you please leave me alone?"

"Just give me a quarter."

"Get out of here," Kip said, giving him a dime and shoving him off.

"I'm really at a loss what to do for you guys," John said to me. "Kip?"

"You could press charges and we could take him in if you want," Kip said to me.

"That won't do any good," I said. "His dog should be picked up by the ASPCA and tested for rabies. That way we won't have to take the shots ourselves."

"You're not taking my dog there," Jersey said. "He can't even stand being cooped up in my apartment."

"I'll call in," John said. He tried his two-way radio. It didn't work.

"Don't look at me, buddy," Kip said. "Mine's in the repair shop."

"I'll call from the pay phone." I went with John to the drugstore across the street. While he phoned I bought a bottle of iodine, applied it to my wounds and then, back on the island, to Milos's ankle.

A squad car came with its siren going and emergency lights twirling. "You buzzed?" the sergeant said from the car.

"We want to know what to do about the dog," John said.

"You should have asked the desk for that." He contacted the station house on the car radio. The station house said "Normal procedure, with or without a dog license, is for ASPCA to take the mutt and quarantine it for seven days. I'll get them over."

We waited. The station house called back a few minutes later and said the ASPCA drivers were on strike. "You fellows will have to bring the dog to the pound yourselves."

"He's not getting in my car without a cage," the sergeant told the station house.

"Hold on." Later: "No cages. All borrowed at one time or another, since no real need for them till now. We can get one by tonight. Take the dog owner's name and address and tell him we'll pick up the dog at nine sharp tomorrow when we have a cage."

"He won't give the right address," I said to the sergeant.

"Also get the names and addresses of an immediate family member and his present employer," the sergeant said to Kip.

"They're all be phonies," I said.

Jersey said to Kip "I don't work now but I'll give you three genuine addresses which I have the papers to prove them: my own, my mother's and my best friend's where I usually stay."

"Which one will you be at tomorrow at nine when we come to pick your dog up?"

"My mother."

"You be there now, you hear?" the sergeant said from the car.

"I promise. My mother's a good woman. Not like me. I swear by everything holy and her name that I'll be there at nine with my dog."

"Bull," I said.

"Faggot," he said to me. "You'll never get anything from anyone around here from now on. I'll tell them. 'Pull in your asses when you see him,' I'll say. 'That faggot's dangerous and mean.'—Can I go now?" he asked Kip.

"Let him loose," the sergeant said.

Jersey walked away with his dog. His friends remained on the bench, talking about movies now: which ones they liked or disliked. The sergeant had said he'd drive Milos and me to a hospital, but suddenly his twirling lights and siren were on and he drove off.

"They were supposed to take us to emergency," I said to John.

"I could get another squad car for you, but it might take a while. You'll be better off by bus."

"We have to go to the hospital and be treated now," I said to Milos.

"Yoicher hyper caper."

I jabbed at myself while I nodded, made a cross in the air and pointed downtown. He looked confused. I hailed a cab and urged Milos to get in with me. During the ride I asked the driver if he'd ever heard this language before and I said to Milos "Say something. Speak. Hospital. L'hopital, Milos," and I pointed downtown and to my wounds and his bad ankle and nodded and he said "Yoicher caper hyper hyper" and the driver said "No, I never have."

Milos and I went to the admitting window of the emergency room of the hospital and I told the man there "We were both bitten by the same mangy dog and would like to be treated for possible rabies right away."

He gave us forms to fill out and bring back to him when we were finished.

We sat in the crowded waiting room. One man waiting to be treated must have been in a razor or knife fight. His cheek and neck were slashed, blood was all over his head and clothes. Seeing me looking at him, the man beside him said "Window fell on his head. No joke. Second-story window, smash, frame and all down on us both, but it got him like in a horseshoe game and only grazed my arm." Another woman must have run into a nest of bees. I don't know where in this city. Maybe she kept her own hives. And a baby with a swelled-up belly and a young girl with towels wrapped around both hands. I filled out my form, took my wallet out and removed some identification papers and pointed to Milos's pocket and he did the same. All his papers were written in letters I didn't recognize. Then I saw a business card of a Hungarian restaurant on the East Side. "You Hungarian?" I said.

"Hungarian."

I said to the waiting room "Anyone here speak Hungarian?"

A woman stood up. "I don't," she said.

Several people laughed.

"But I'm Finnish," she said.

This time even a few of the sick and injured people laughed.

"But the two languages are somewhat alike. They're both branches of the Finno-Ugric."

"The Finno-whatwik?" a man said and just about everyone laughed.

"Then I need you here, ma'am," I said when the noise had died down. She came over and talked to Milos and they seemed to understand many of the words the other one spoke and she helped him fill out his form.

Two men came in holding up a third. They sat him down. One of the men went to the admitting window and said "My friend there's been shot."

"Have you seen a policeman?" the admitting man said.

"It happened right in front of the hospital just now. Didn't you hear the blast?"

"No. You should have summoned a policeman before you came in."

"Hey Jack," he yelled, "they want us to get a policeman first."

Jack, sitting beside the wounded man, said "They're crazy. First treatment, then a policeman."

"First treatment, then a policeman, my friend says."

"Can the person who's shot fill out the admitting form?"

"He's bleeding to death, probably dying. He got it in the stomach. We thought we were lucky that it happened in front of your place."

"You can fill it out then, but you'll be responsible for the twenty-dollar admitting fee."

"I don't write but Jack does, and between us we don't have twenty cents."

"Fee temporarily waived then," and he stamped something on the form. "But your friend Jack must put his address and signature here so we can mail him the bill."

A woman came in with a burnt arm and back. Her hair was singed. A path was cleared for her when she walked to the window and a few people held their noses as she passed. The admitting man said "Yes?" She tried to speak. She fell to the floor. He called for two aides over the public address system. They came out of the swinging doors in back and put her on a stretcher and carried her inside.

"What about our rabies?" I said, giving the admitting man our completed forms. "For all we know we can be getting it now, and once you do you've had it I understand."

"Excuse me." He took the form from Jack and told him to take the man who was shot into the examining room. Jack and his friend helped the man in and then left.

"Now," the admitting man said to me, "were either of you bitten on the head or face?"

"No."

"Splenius, sternocleidomstoid, anywhere near the larynx or voice box?"

"I was bitten twice on the calf and the Hungarian man once on the ankle. And the skin broke in all three bites and the dog's saliva got in."

"The incubation period for your types of bites is rarely less than fifteen days and I guarantee you'll be in the examining room by then."

I asked the Finnish woman to tell Milos what the man had just said. She again left her father in the care of a stranger sitting beside him and spoke to Milos. He shook his head and began repeating something to her.

"He's apparently saying the incubation period might be for fifteen days. But you have to take virus injections in the stomach for fourteen days starting from the day you were bitten, which leaves you both with only one day left, he says, and conceivably he about ten minutes fewer than you."

I told the admitting man what Milos had said.

"So you have one day left. You still won't be waiting here that long. Even the chances of a dog getting rabies in this city are practically nonexistent, so please sit down."

We waited another hour. The child with the swollen belly and the man with the cut face and the father of the Finnish lady were taken before us. Then the beebite lady and Milos and I were called. We sat in one of the examining rooms with four other patients, all on stools in a circle, my knees touching the knees of the Finnish man whose daughter, standing behind him and holding his hand, said he'd come in to get a splinter removed that she had dug and dug at but couldn't even reach. A woman was telling a man with a bad cough of the beautiful mad golden retriever that had bitten her this morning.

"That's a coincidence," I said, "for I was bitten too."

"Same here," the beebite lady said.

"Both of you by golden retrievers?" the woman said.

"No, a pack of bees."

"Mine was a mutt. But yours couldn't have been on Broadway in the eighties, was it?"

"Connecticut."

"I wish I only got bit by a dog in Connecticut," the beebite lady said, "or at least only by one bee. But hundreds. Right on West Fifty-first in the heart of the restaurant district when I'm out dumping my garbage bag."

The woman said she was driving in on the thruway when she saw a car ride off the road right in front of her and turn over a couple of times before it came up on its wheels. "I parked. A few cars got there before me and someone said the driver looked dead but that there was a dog on the seat who wouldn't let them open the door to help the man. All the windows were shattered. I tried coaxing the dog out. I've a way with them and especially retrievers—I've two myself. When it wouldn't come with words I held a strip of beef jerky through the window to get him to sniff it and eventually follow it out of the car with me, but he bit my hand."

A nurse asked each of us our medical problems and assigned the beebite lady and the cut man to special rooms. The man with the cough was given a throat swab and a prescription and told to come back tomorrow for the results. A doctor came in, gave the rest of us tetanus shots, washed our wounds and while the nurse prepared the Finnish man for minor surgery, bandaged us up and asked about the dogs that bit us.

Mina, the woman, said she'd phoned Connecticut just before and was told the retriever was licensed, had had all his shots and was now quarantined, and the doctor said the vets there will know if the dog shows any clinical signs of rabies within seven days. "What about your dogs?" he asked Milos and me.

"It has no license and probably never had any shots or will ever be found," I said and he told me if the dog isn't confined in two days we should return to this hospital and begin taking our fixed virus shots.

"I hear they can be very painful," I said.

"And possible severe reactions to the treatment can happen, so in actual fact we don't recommend them."

"But if we get rabies we can go into convulsions and die."

"There hasn't been a reported case of rabies bite in the city for over thirty years."

"Maybe this is the one. Or the man and his dog were from out of town and only visiting here for the day."

"There weren't a hundred reported cases in the entire country last year and most of those attacking rabid animals weren't dogs."

"What would you do?" I asked him.

"I'd take the injections," Mina said.

"I wouldn't," he said. "Though in the end that comes down to a personal and not a professional decision, so I know how tough it must be for both of you."

"I'll make up my mind in two days." I got Milos's phone number and said to the Finnish woman "Tell him I'll call in two days to report if the dog's been found. If it hasn't, say he'll then have to speak to his own people and make up his own mind on whether he wants to go through with the virus shots."

Mina, Milos and I went to a coffee shop nearby. I told Mina I'd like to take her out for dinner one night this week and she said "I don't think it'd be too good an idea as I'm sort of seeing someone now."

"But we've had too inauspicious and eventful and coincidental a beginning not to see what develops next."

"I wouldn't go that far. But I don't suppose a single dinner with you can matter that much and we can also learn how we all made out with our bites." She gave me her phone number. The three of us shook hands and took separate buses home.

I called the police station the next day and the man at the desk said the first address Jersey gave was fake and they're now trying to run him down at either his own apartment or where he said his friend lives.

"This is a real emergency," I said. "As even the injection treatments for rabies can sometimes be fatal, so this other man and I want to avoid them at all costs."

I called the station the next day and the policeman said "All three addresses were fake and we don't know what else to do for you now."

"I know where Jersey and his type hang out."

"You one of them?"

"No, I just live in the neighborhood and walk around a lot. And I see that on the island across from Loews 83rd is where a lot of the transvestites like to hang out these days, though every other month or so they switch to another island a block or two north or south."

"If you see him let us know," and he gave me a special number to call.

I went to the island on Broadway. One of the transvestites of two days ago was sitting alone on a bench.

"Excuse me," I said, "but do you know where I can find your friend Jersey?"

"I've no friend Jersey. She a friend of yours?"

"Jersey's dog bit me the other day and I'm trying to find it to see if it has rabies."

"Oh sure, now I remember. Bad scene. Too many police."

"Can you tell me where Jersey is?"

"She and her dog are dead."

"No, really."

"No, really, dead. Hit by a car."

"Both killed by the same car? Around here?"

"She didn't die, just her dog. Ballpark, she called him. The dog. Jersey went to California. Picked up on this very corner here by some new queer who stops his car and says 'I love you, darling, what's your name?' And they made it—just like that."

"I could still find out if the dog had rabies if you knew when and where the accident took place and what they might have done with the dog's body."

"Her dog didn't die either. He ran away. Ballpark. Jersey let her go when she got in that rich queer's car. 'Freedom,' she says to Ballpark, 'that's your new name,' and Ballpark runs off."

"Is that the truth now? It's kind of a life and death situation for me that I know."

"I don't know Jersey anymore. I don't want to. She's a mean mother. You saw. Lie and cheat, cheat and lie. I hate them all. And all her friends too, rich or poor."

"Can you at least tell me where she was staying or give me the name and address of someone who might know?"

"No. No one knows. And if I see her I don't speak to her or say hello. I'll say nothing. I'll walk past. Besides, I hear she's gone to Las Vegas for good with a gambler who gave up his

wife and kids for her and now only likes gays. A laugh. Because
Jersey's no gay. That's true."

I called Mina that night.

"I'm sorry," she said, "but Lewis who?"

"The fellow who was bitten by a dog the same day as you."

"Of course. You know, I told that story about us to my
roommate and she said that only happens in movies where we
get married the following week and a month later regret racing
into it and have major calamities and breakups together but live
happily ever after for life, though of course she was only kidding.
How are your bites?"

"They haven't found the dog."

"That's terrible. Mine's healing nicely. And so far the dog
seems okay and I'm even planning to adopt it, since that poor
car driver was crippled and can't take care of it anymore. You
going to take those treatments? It's been two days."

"I think I'll wait it out. Would you like to have dinner with
me tonight?"

"I'm afraid that person I said I'm sort of seeing I'm sort of
engaged to now, so I don't think I can."

"I'll call back next week to find out about your dog and you.
Maybe by then you'll also have changed your mind about me."

"I don't think so, but thanks."

The police never found Jersey or the dog. I called Mina again
after our incubation period for rabies was over and her roommate
answered and said "Mina? That rat skipped off on her honeymoon to Bermuda and left me with her two stinking retrievers
and a third one that bites people coming any day. Who is this?"

"Lewis."

"Of the dogs?"

"Yes."

"She left a message for you, Lewis, that she told me to read
to you if you call again. It says 'I didn't know your phone
number nor last name so I couldn't call you with what I forgot

to remind you about the last time you called. I was also in too much of a rush to get off on my honeymoon trip to wait the two days the hospital said it would take to locate your records. But I want to make sure, if that dog that bit you isn't found, that you phone the Hungarian man to tell him a lot of people would think it advisable for him to take the ten to fourteen day vaccine treatment for rabies.' That's it. So long."

I'd completely forgotten about Milos. I called the restaurant number he gave me and the man who answered said "No Milos, sir—tonight. Can't speak English please. Tonight."

I called back that night and the restaurant owner said "Milos is in the kitchen now washing the dishes. He's doing a fine job here and not suffering any rabies or illnesses we can see. Want me to have him phone you back?"

"No thanks."

Buddy

Today was a day of meeting people I know.

My Christmas job was over till next year. I finished another sonata last night. I didn't feel like looking for work just yet or starting another composition or hanging around the house all day cleaning, doing the laundry, shopping for groceries, none of that. So I slept late, had coffee, browsed through the who's-who-in-contemporary-music book while the eggs boiled, and after breakfast decided to take a walk downtown.

The first person I met was the old man from the first floor. It was right outside our building. He beeped his horn. I turned and saw him in his parked car, the windows up and motor running. He often sat there like that, reading, singing, sleeping, not doing much. In the eight years I've lived here I've never seen him with another person. He rolled down his window and said "You get any heat today?"

"Some."

"Boy, my place is an icebox. Can't understand it. We're all fed from the same boiler and pipes. That's why I'm here. And last night my fuse blew and the box is in the locked basement and the landlady wasn't answering her phone. After sleeping with an electric blanket for fifteen years, I couldn't get in three winks. So what, right? And getting too cold for me. See ya," and he rolled up his window.

The next people I met were from the block and immediate neighborhood. I must be acquainted with a couple of hundred people from around here including neighbors, supers, kids playing, shopkeepers, city service people, people from the bars and stores and the local street winos and summer domino people and the like. The seven or eight I met till I finally got out of the neighborhood I either smiled or waved to or said "Hey, how's it going?" and they said "Fine" and I said "Good" or they said "How are you?" and I said "Fine" and they said "Good" and that was our conversation. Occasionally when I've said "How's it going?" someone would stop to tell me. Usually it was the blues. Today the only person who stopped me was the owner of several remodeled brownstones on the block. I nodded as I passed. She grabbed my arm and said "Those people."

"I looked around and said "What people?"

"Those people. There. Look at them," and she ripped a sign off the lamppost which said there was going to be a block party with guitar entertainment at the corner church one week from tonight: free admission, bring cookies, wine and soda sold. She'd been in a Nazi death camp and had numbers on her arm and a few times had told me how the Russian soldiers liberated a boxcar of women she was in and raped all of them and shot half of them and shaved off all their body hairs and carved Cyrillic letters into their montes veneris and heads. She said, tearing the sign in two, "All these committees are nothing but pseudoliberal gudgeons or Reds."

"Who knows," I said, "and try and have a nice day."

The first person I recognized outside my neighborhood was someone I went to school with at Music and Art and Juilliard. He was entering a bank. I yelled out his name. He didn't hear me. I followed him in and joined him on the teller's line. "Hey, Enos."

"Buddy old boy," and he kissed my cheek. "God you look good. What's new? Still in their pitching?"

"No sell or soap though. But you're strong. Mr. Jingle, name up in brights."

"Let me tell you about it."

"Great if it's what you like. How's Lola?"

"Where you been? She unloaded me for my lyricist and took the girls. Third page in the *Post*. Don't you read anything but scores? I'm with a new chickadee now. Young. Great flautist. Really does those scales. Comes from a fine family of virtuoso pipers that go back to Prince Kinsky and Rasoumou. And anti-marriage and big knockers that Lola never had. Remember? Flat, like everything else about her. I'm going to snap a time shot montage of those tits with me blowing and playing on them and send it to Lo just to make her seat sweat. You married?"

"Nah."

"Teaching?"

"Those kids were nuts. Throwing the music stands at me, pouring mucilage between the keys. Screw it. Even for money I wasn't going insane."

"Try college."

"No master's."

"Get a master's."

"No stomach for going back to school."

"Find a stomach. What about private lessons?"

"Some people teach," I started to say, but the teller said "Next." Enos waved a fistful of checks at me and went up to the teller and said "This one I'd like in cash, the rest deposited." I told him I had to run. He said "Wait, we got to get together. At my place for dinner one night or one of the old bars. You listed?"

"No phone."

"Still rebelling?"

"No afford. Deposit's too high. Those rings. Bad tone. They don't fit in my small room. And stuff the bell up with tissues and I don't know when someone calls."

"Then reach me through my agent." He gave me a card. "Be speaking to you, Bud."

A few blocks further downtown I saw one of my father's old friends.

"Mr. Landau," I said.

"Sorry, I don't quite catch you."

"Ira Quiver's son, Buttinsky. How are you?"

"Buddy. It's been a long time. How's dad?"

"He died last month."

"How's mother taking it?"

"She died three years ago."

"Sorry to hear that. Good seeing you again. Regards home."

"You too to Mrs. Landau and stay well."

I watched him go. My father and he were very close. They used to kick the can and get in the movies two-for-five together on the Lower East Side. The day my father died I called him and gave the time and place of the funeral. It was in the neighborhood. I live a few blocks from the building I grew up in and where my folks lived the last forty years of their lives. He didn't come. A month ago I got a condolence card from his wife saying "Lou forgot and never told me and I avoid the obits like the plague. He hasn't been in his right mind these past years. He started to forget his name and address and who his wife is the day your father first got so seriously ill. Sometimes he tells me he wants to visit Ira and Liz and the kids, and sneaks out when the cook's not looking and for a day and night nobody knows where he is. If you ever see him on the street or buzzing the bells of your parents' old building, please put him in a cab and personally deliver him home."

A few blocks farther downtown I saw one of the women I worked with at my Christmas job in a department store. She was across the avenue, separated from me by a lot of traffic, walking in her very distinctive way past Philharmonic Hall. Her height, singer's chest and quick dignified walk were how I could pick her out in the crowd from so far away. We'd sold men's pajamas. During the slower moments we talked about music, recordings, love, sex and the stage. She told me she was studying to be an opera and operetta singer and one time asked me to explain how I liked having it done with the lips and tongue as a few of her boyfriends complained she didn't do it excitingly enough for them though none could pinpoint what was wrong. I asked her to demonstrate how she did it. She turned her back to the main floor customers, voyeurs and exhibitionists flitting past and did these rapid up-and-down motions with her tongue. I said it looked like a paddlewheel working at breakneck speed. I suggested she move it slower, like an oar of a rowboat piloted by a one-armed lethargic oarsman in calm waters with no express place to go, and see one of the raunchier porno flicks that were all over town: the best cost five bucks. She said she'd seen the best and doing it their way especially with one of her boyfriends would ravage her vocal cords. "Those cords come first in my life," she said, "so I don't want them cut or touched." I ran across the avenue against the light and tapped her shoulder.

"Hi," she said. "How weird seeing one of my coworkers," as we were called, "outside the store. You like to walk?"

"Love it."

"Besides singing I like to do it more than anything. And on these raw days, almost more."

"What do you like to do more on these raw days?"

"Don't horse me."

"You mean you like to do that too?"

"You'd think with our musical background and education we'd have much more to say."

We walked uptown. It was a grind keeping up with her. She had long legs and a big gait and was taller, taller than I and

I'm tall, besides wearing platform shoes that hoisted her a half foot more. She was also beautiful and people stared, several drivers honked their horns at her and one trucker even rolled down his window in this weather to whistle. Things like that still went on. I actually pictured her practicing this walk nude with these shoes on and a glass of water on top of a book balanced on her head.

We passed most of the places I'd recently passed. The bus stop Mr. Landau was still waiting at. I waved. He licked his fingertip and held it above his head to learn something about the wind. "I know that man," I said, "honest."

And Enos coming out of a high-priced men's store with clothes boxes. "Two times in twenty minutes is kind of pushing it," he said. He stared at Carla and winked that man-to-man wink at me and hailed a cab. I winked back at him and my eyelids got stuck.

"Who's that?" she said.

"Fiddler I know."

"What's with your eye? Never met anyone who could hold a tic that long." I pried my eyelids apart. "That's better. He looked prosperous. I like prosperous men. All creative and performing types have just about the same thing going for them, so why not one who's rich?"

"Beats me. And I'm cold. I'd like a hot chocolate or just to head home."

"Your place? You could show me something for voice you've done."

"You wouldn't like my closet. Too raw. I've lieder based on passages from German sex manuals, but you'd be too chilled to sing them and I've no piano."

"I've got hot water and a pot."

She lived a few blocks away. I sat in her living room. She had a grand piano, perfectly tuned. When I wanted to play I subwayed to other boroughs or pretended to be a customer in a piano store. I went through a movement of last night's sonata while she made hot chocolate in the kitchen. "That's nice," she said, "but it can't be sung as nobody has that range." I told her it was written for kit violin and contrabassoon.

"All serious geniuses are self-destructive and ultimately boring," she said. "You ought to give your fiddler friend my number and name."

I devised an elaborate plan of getting into bed with her, starting with wandering through the ancient instrument rooms at the art museum and then drinks, dinner, coffee at an espresso house whose jukebox only played opera overtures and arias and barcaroles, and then a cab home. She passed through the room chumping on a thick sandwich and sipping the only hot chocolate and from the bedroom said "Listen, composer, I've a voice lesson in an hour and acting and fencing classes after that, so if we want to make it a duet we better do it right now."

She had an upright in the bedroom, also perfectly tuned. She took off her clothes and went into the bathroom. I took off my clothes and played a new melody that was in my head. "Hey," she yelled, "tinkle something madrigalian for me in here."

There was a harpsichord opposite the toilet. I sat on the toilet seat cover and played a madrigal by Gesualdo while she hummed along as she swabbed her underarms and genitals with a washrag. I said "If you take a lot of these steamy stand-ups and hot showers, you could ruin your plectra and keys."

"Come here," she said, and still with her back to me, grabbed my penis from behind, vised it between her thighs and sort of gave it a shoeshine with the washrag. Then she leaned forward, popped me in, clutched the two towel racks on either side of the sink and right at the end of her lovemaking broke out into several bars from Lucia's Mad Scene but the peak in high coloratura F instead of Donizetti's original E-flat.

"You've a very fine voice," I said, "though I don't see you singing this way on stage."

"You'd be surprised. Gets me an octave higher. And they do it now in modern ballet and Broadway musicals. And how else do you think American opera's going to survive once the great patrons pass away and if the national endowment funds don't rise? But you better get. My voice teacher comes here."

"That was fun. Can I call you sometime?"

"I see other men, so I get enough. Including two big bassos who I'm even in love with, so it's only like every so often when I'm suddenly horny and the opportunity presents itself that I make use of it, and today you were one of those. Bye-bye."

She put on her bathrobe and threw me my socks. We kissed for the first time when I had one foot out the front door. I put my arm around her and with the other hand twiddled her nipple, first time for those two too. She said "Come on, let up, I want you out of here allegro, as I also have these pre-lesson thoracic exercises to do."

I left, headed downtown again. In the theater district I saw my brother leaving a movie house. He didn't see me. Last year he said not seeing me for the rest of his life would be just enough time. Curious thing was that the previous evening I dreamt of us bumping into each other on a cloud in heaven and giving him my finished sonata to read and possibly orchestrate and he telling me to shove off. The reason for all that was because Clark thought I should have acted sooner in calling a doctor for our father. Clark was living in Cincinnati then. I was sleeping almost every night at my father's apartment. A private nurse stayed days with my father while I worked at two crummy jobs to pay her. One night my father complained of pains in his chest. I said it must be the knockwurst I'd told him not to eat for dinner and gave him two antacid tablets. I think I called him a big baby when he continued to complain. He told me to dummy up and phone the doctor. I said "What the hell will a doctor do for you: you've only got gas. I'll phone and he'll tell me to call an ambulance. You'll be in the hospital for two weeks undergoing tests. You'll end up with bed sores as big as grapefruits and possibly pneumonia because of your inactivity there and because of that maybe die." He said I had a point and I gave him belladonna drops in water and told him to call it a night. Early next morning he got a heart attack and died in the hospital the same day. That was when Clark flew in and said he was disowning me for life. Because he's older and we were now orphans and he was the sole benefactor of our father's small estate, I suppose he could say that. Now he was walking with a young girl. It could be my niece. Clark and his wife were musicologists and conductors of little orchestra and choral groups and because they couldn't stand the names Polyhymnia and Euterpe, named their only child Clio.

I followed them for a block. As they were going into a chili place I said "Hi, Clio."

"Hello," she said, "but who are you?"

Clark pulled her into the restaurant. I said "Oh well."

Walking farther downtown I met in succession a grade school teacher of mine who asked if I'd become the miracle physician I swore I would, an old boss who wanted to know if I'd come to no good as a glazier and served the prison sentence he prophesied the day he fired me, a former roommate who asked if I was still chiseling wizened landladies out of rent and beating out on loans and lost bets with good friends and being evicted from apartments because my playing was unremitting and too loud. Then I saw Lettie. It was near the southern tip of the city. She teaches film-making at an upstate high school but for some reason was leading a class up the Stock Exchange Building steps. She was with a man. They were holding hands. Lettie was the woman I'd been seeing every weekend for two years and spent last summer with attending concerts and visiting dead composers' homes in Europe. I'd wanted to marry and move in with her and compose at home while finding part-time work in her area, but she said that after talking blue flames in class all day all she wanted was to come home to her plants, highstrung son and singing birds.

I yelled "Lettie." She turned to me, took her hand out of the man's. I climbed the steps, kissed her cheek.

"Bud, this is Dom." We shook hands. "Dom asked me to help chaperon his economics class today. I had a light work load, so it was easy shifting my classes around to come."

Dom's class was standing at the entrance to the building. "I think we have to get up there," she said to me.

"I'll take care of them for a while," Dom said. "Nice to meet you, Bud," and he left.

"That your new beau?"

"I see Dom from time to time."

"Does it ever get further than the hand?"

"Please don't ask silly questions."

"You never mentioned him."

"I don't see why I had to."

"You never mentioned anyone else."

"Dom's the only other one."

"He seems like a nice fellow."

"You can't tell in so short a time. But he's nice, though different than you in many ways you wouldn't like. He hates classical music and cracks up at operas."

"It's been a day of coincidences for me, meeting you and so many other people I know."

"With you everything's a coincidence. Your associative powers can get a bit much for me. Sometimes I don't believe you."

"We're not getting along very well this minute."

"What do you expect?"

"Do you make it with Dom?"

"Sure we make it. What do you expect?"

"You never told me."

"This is also a day of repetitions for you. Anyway, you must have other women during the week."

"No one."

"You should. You're talented. If you ever get fed up with all the frustrations inherent in composing, you could probably survive all right passing around the other stuff."

"Will I see you this weekend?"

"Not this weekend. Maybe the next."

"I don't think I like our arrangement anymore."

"Then I guess we have to decide against having any arrangement."

"It's decided then."

"Done." I put out my hand to shake. She said "Oh yes, shaking. That's about the one physical thing I haven't done with you. Now I can say I did everything I ever wanted to do with you, except teasing your hair. Goodbye."

She went upstairs. I walked to the tip of the city where the ferry stations are. I didn't meet anyone else I know. I took the subway home, bought a bottle of wine, got sleepy reading while finishing the bottle, sang lots of familiar airs to my own non-sensical words as I usually do when I get high, and went to bed.

Grace Calls

Grace calls. Grace called. I stand. I sit. I go to bed. I dream. I dream about my childhood. I dream about my birth. I dream about being an old man. I wake. Grace calls. Grace called. I make breakfast. I eat. I go to the bathroom. I read. I wash. I make lunch. I eat. I drink a glass of water. I read. I listen to the radio. I make a sandwich. I eat. I drink a glass of milk. I put water on for coffee. I read. I smell something burning. It's the tea kettle on the stove. I open the window to let out the smoke. I watch a pigeon feather float in and land on the floor. I close the window. I throw away the burnt kettle. I sit. I read. I make supper. I eat. I wash the dishes. I put the trash outside the front door. I run in place. I shave. I bathe. I read. I drink a glass of beer. I read. I listen to the radio. I make a snack. I eat. I read. I undress. I go to bed. I think about what I did today. I think about what I dreamt last time I slept. I think about my father. I see him waving at me and saying "Juney boy." I think about my mother. She's in an evening gown coming downstairs. She's sitting on the sill washing my window. She's in a suit going to work. She's in her doctor's coat examining someone's ear. A boy's ear. My ear. I'm sitting on her examining table and she's examining me with that instrument that has a light. She says "No good." She says "Stick out your tongue." She says "Just what I thought." She says "Sit still while I make a call." She comes back with her receptionist and says "You must be a brave boy now, you mustn't be afraid." I fall asleep. I dream about eggplants. They're purple, with faces, and my size. I'm running down a steep hill with a slew of them on my way to see our housekeeper Anna. We cross a country road. One eggplant stays on the other side of the road and all the eggplants and I move our heads for it to cross the road. It bounces across the road on its bottom and gets hit by a big car. The car keeps going. Hit and run, I say. We drag the eggplant off the road and form a circle around it and talk about its qualities and weaknesses and cover it with dirt and most of us cry. I wake. I go to the bathroom. I wipe sweat off my face and back. I drink water from the tap. I go back to bed. I think about what my eggplant dream could have meant. And where is Anna now and what hill was that I ran down? I fall asleep. I dream. I dream of my father treating me in his office. His waiting room's filled as it was always filled with patients and friends. He says "Say ah." He says "Spit it out." I lean over the dental bowl and spit out pieces of an old filling and blood. He says "Now sit back and open wide." He says "Wider." He says "Wider." I watch him look through his thick bifocals at what he's drilling and picking at. He says "All done." He sticks cotton rolls in my mouth and says "Keep it open till I fill it." He mashes and mixes my future silver filling in his porcelain mortar with his porcelain pestle. A man comes into the treatment room and says "Doc, got a moment?" I wake. Grace calls. Grace called. I dress. I run in place. I put water on for coffee. I go to the bathroom. I read. I smell something burning. I see smoke passing the bathroom door. I flush the toilet. The water pot burnt. A kitchen wall's on fire. I try putting the fire out with water I spray from the sink tap. The doorbell rings. Several neighbors come and help me put out the fire. The landlord comes. He speaks to the neighbors. I mop the floor. The neighbors leave. The landlord says "That's your third fire in five weeks. The other two weren't that serious, but this one is. I'm going to get an eviction notice out on you immediately, so don't bother paying next month's rent." The landlord leaves. I hang the mop and rags out to dry. I close the window. The landlord returns. He says "Forget what I said about not paying next month's rent. You pay it, all right, and all the other months till I get you thrown out." He leaves. I read. Grace calls. Grace called. I put water on for coffee. I throw away the burnt pot. I stand by the stove till the water boils. I make breakfast. I eat. I read. I drink coffee. I get the newspaper off my doormat. I read. I reheat the coffee. I stand by the stove till the coffee's reheated. I drink coffee. I read. I make lunch. I eat. I drink a glass of water. I brush my teeth. I look out the window. A boy kicks a can into the street. A car passes. A taxi drops off its passenger. The postman delivers mail. A woman walks her dog. A delivery boy rides by on a bike. A man walks past holding an opened umbrella over his head though it isn't raining or sunny. It's cloudy and the temperature's mild. A sanitation truck picks up garbage. A man yells "Hey you. Stop thief." Another man runs up the block toward the park with the first man's brown paper bag. A police car comes. The policemen talk to the man who lost the bag. The man gets in the police car and the police car goes. A man and woman walk by holding hands. They stop. He ties his shoelaces. They kiss. They go. They stop, kiss, go. A woman dressed in white with white makeup on her face and neck and her hair powdered white and shoes polished white and everything on her like her nail polish and hands and ears painted or made white though she's black, walks past. Only the shopping cart she's lugging behind her isn't white. It's aluminum, though its one wheel and all the wheel's spokes and the axle are white. The two filled shopping bags in the cart and material and packages she has over the bags are white. I don't know what she means. She has breasts so large and round that it could be she isn't a woman but is a circus clown with balloons or whatever they use to make it seem like they have enormous breasts stuffed under their costumes. But she's a woman, or she isn't a woman. Sparks fly from the sidewalk where the wheelless side of the axle drags. The postman watches her and smiles to himself as he unstrings a bundle of mail. I still don't know what she means. There could be several meanings. I have to go to the bathroom. I get a glass of water. I return to the window. Two motor scooters go past. The drivers ride side by side and the two helmeted passengers holding on in back talk to one another. The woman of white is now at the avenue end of the block, still dragging the cart. I recall the intense look to keep going that never left her face. I still don't know what she means. A black woman. Or perhaps not a woman but a man made up to look like a woman. But a black man made up to look like a white woman, but a woman in white leotards and white walking shoes and enormous breasts and possibly a stuffed enormous behind and lugging a filled shopping cart with only the basket part of this one-wheeled cart not painted white and with light panties under the leotard and a white undershirt over it and with every visible part of the cart's contents and her body except the irises made or being white. Grace calls. I don't answer. I drink the water. I go to the bathroom. I pour milk into the water glass. I sip once from the glass and pour the milk back into the container and return the container to the refrigerator. I read. I feed my plant. I listen to the radio. I run in place. I sweep the rug. I dust some shelves. I sit. I read. I nap. I dream of something that actually happened when I was three. It was my birthday. I was very small for my age. Too small to climb onto my parents' double bed without someone's help. I thought they must use a ladder to get on their bed. I visualized a ladder against the side of the bed. I ask them to help me get up on the bed. They don't understand my words as I wasn't able to make a single word understandable to adults till I was past four.

I put out my arms in the direction of the bed. My father picks me up and drops me on the bed. He takes a pillow and swipes me lightly on the head. As far as my memory goes, the real incident ends. The dream goes on. My mother complains my father's messing up the newly made bed. He lifts me off the bed, looks for a place to set me and puts me in my mother's arms. He folds the bedspread back over the pillow, straightens the bed, goes to the kitchen, puts his sandwich and tangerine into a manila envelope, kisses my mother and I goodbye and leaves for work. My mother says "Happy birthday, sweetheart, you're three." She says "From your father and me." She gives me a wrapped present. I can't get the ribbon off. She opens it. It's a dog doll. She kisses my ear and goes to work in her office at the front of the house. I play with the ribbon and wrapping in the room Anna's ironing in. The dream ends. I wake up. Grace calls. Grace called. I go to the bathroom. I read. I shave. I clean the toilet bowl and tub. I look in the mirror. I tweeze the hair out of my nose. I part my hair in the middle and pretend I'm someone else. I brush my hair back the way I always wear it. I work on the crossword puzzle. I check the movie listings. I put water on for coffee. I stand at the stove till the water boils. I make lunch. I eat. I drink coffee. I make a snack. I eat. I peel a carrot. I eat. I look through the cookbook. Grace calls. I don't answer. Grace calls. Grace called. I look out the window. Across the street a woman in the second-story apartment directly opposite mine is looking at an oil truck delivering oil to her building. The oilman reels in the hose and the truck leaves. I stare at the woman. She looks at me. I smile and wave. She leaves her window seat. I look up and down the street. I can't see a person, animal or vehicle moving on the block. Curtains move in one of the buildings across the street and now a sheet of newspaper moves in the street but nothing else. The leaves on the block's tree move. A sparrow flies out of the tree and disappears over the row of buildings on my side of the block. A man comes out of a building reading a magazine. He pats his pockets. "Darn," he seems to say. He goes back into his building. Several children on rollerskates and with hockey sticks pass. A car passes. A bus. I've never seen a bus come down this sidestreet. Maybe the street the bus usually goes down is blocked up. The man leaves the building again carrying a briefcase and with the magazine under his arm. The bus stops a few doors down from my building. The car in front of it is double-parked too far from the car parked adjacent to the curb and the bus can't get past. The bus driver honks. His passengers read, talk, look outside, one's asleep. The bus driver and the drivers of the two cars and a truck behind the cars honk. A woman comes out of a building. She jiggles her keys to the bus driver. He honks. She points to her watch and raises her shoulders and hands. The bus driver and the drivers of the cars and the truck behind the cars honk. She gets in the double-parked car and drives off. The bus starts for the corner right after her but has to stop for the light. The woman just made it through the light. The bus and car and truck drivers honk and honk. Grace calls. Grace called. I drink a glass of water. I go to the door. The afternoon paper's on the mat. I throw the paper away. I reheat the coffee. I do exercises and run in place. I wash my hands and face. The pot's burning. I put out the fire. I throw the pot through the window. The police come. One policeman says "Your landlord called to complain. First fires, he says. Now deliberately destroying his property." I hear honking from the street. I go to the window. The policeman says "When I'm talking to you you don't move." The driver of another bus is honking the double-parked police car in front of my building. I point to the street. The policeman says "What now, for god-sakes?" He looks outside. He says "I'll take care of our car, you take care of him." He leaves. The second policeman says "Why you do these things we don't know. You've a nice place. Nice and neat. Plenty of room. It's a good building. Your landlord seems like a nice enough guy. It's a nice street and good neighborhood. You're lucky to live here, believe me, and from what I hear, you're getting it cheap. So no more fuss now, please." He leaves. I go to the window. The bus is gone. The police car's backing into a parking spot. The policeman who just left my place taps the police car's roof. The car stops. He gets inside. The car drives out of the spot and goes through the red light. Several people across the street have come to their windows. Some are looking at me. I smile at the woman sitting on the window seat. She lets down her venetian blinds and flicks them shut. I drink water from the kitchen tap. I let the water run to get cold. Grace calls. Grace called. I see water trickling out of the kitchen. In the kitchen I see I've caused a small flood. I shut the water off. The fire department comes. They drag a hose through my place. The fire chief says to these men "No need." He says to me "For the safety of all your neighbors, you ought to be locked up." They leave. I get the mop from outside the window. Someone knocks. I mop. The landlord says "This is your landlord, Mr. Lingley, open up." I mop. He says "I said open up." I open the door. He says "I've called the police and department of buildings and mayor's office. If you aren't out by tomorrow morning I'll be very much surprised." He leaves. I lock the door. He says from the stairway "Remember what I said last time about your paying next month's rent? Don't." Grace calls. I drink a glass of beer. I hang the mop over the bathtub. I cut my hair. Grace calls. I run in place. I eat a celery stick. I hear music. I go to the window. A street band's passing. I haven't seen one in years. I throw a ball of aluminum foil at it. The flutist salutes me. He opens the foil and shakes his flute at me. I forgot to put money in the foil. I throw two quarters at him. Both coins roll under a parked car. The banjoist says "Thank you, thanks a lot." The violinist hands his violin to the base player and gets down on his knees to retrieve the coins. A car drives by and nearly sideswipes him. The trumpeter blasts his horn at the car. The car honks back repeatedly and makes a turn at the corner. The band resumes playing and walks to the end of the block. I'm leaning out the window to watch them and nearly fall off the ledge. The landlord says from the sidewalk "Don't tell me. You're going to jump. That'll save you the trouble of appearing in court. But jump from someone else's building, as what I don't need now is my insurance rates going up." I climb back inside and slam the window down. It's the window I threw the pot through and it completely shatters from the impact and the glass crashes below. The landlord says "That's it. Out you go today." He runs into the building. I make supper. Police come. I go into the bedroom and eat and drink. Police knock. I lock the bedroom door and try to nap. A policeman yells "Come on now, sir, you've got to unlock." I throw my hairbrush and shoes through the bedroom windows. The landlord yells "Break down the door before he destroys my house." I set fire to my bed and toss the chair and lamps into the flames. Grace calls. The police are banging on the bedroom door. Grace calls. The fire department comes. They enter through the bedroom window this time. They put out the fire on my clothes. They put out the fire in the room. I'm put on a stretcher. Grace calls. I'm carried downstairs. In the street I look up at the window where that woman usually sits and see her leaning outside at me and shaking her head. I'm driven down the block. I see that black man or black woman made up to look like a white woman peering into the ambulance as we go through the red light. I hear the street band play. I pass out. I wake up. I'm in a hospital. I'm in a hospital bed. A tube's in my arm. Another tube takes my pee. Several machines and monitors are at the foot of my bed. One doctor says to another that I've third degree burns over fifty percent of my body and I'm not expected to live. A hospital aide says "Someone by the name of Grace called." A nurse says "You really in great pain?" She gives me something to sleep. I fall asleep. I dream of my parents and my dog Red. My mother says "Red's been taken away." I say "Where away?" My father says "No use lying to you. Big Red's been run over." I say "Where over?" My mother says "She was run over by a steamroller and won't be coming back." I cry. The dream ends. I wake up. That incident never happened in real life. I once did have a dog named Red. She got old and bit me in the face. They had to kill her. I remember when they took her away. They came to our house and put her in a cage. I remember hoping Red would bite them. There was something about her viciousness so late in life that I really liked. But Red was put away. "Where away?" I said. "You still don't know what we mean when we say she's been put away?" my mother said. "No," I said. "Not in a trunk or chest of drawers," my father said. I cried then. I'm lying on my back now in the hospital bed. The food and antibiotic tube's been taken out of my left arm and put in my right. The catheter's still taking my pee. With all the painkillers the nurse says they're giving me, I'm still in great pain. The doctor says "You're improving." The aide says "That person named Grace called just before. What message you want me to give should she call again?" But I can see by their faces that it's hopeless and I fall asleep.

The Village

The man crashed through the second-story window and landed on the sidewalk. He was lucky he wasn't impaled on the iron gate spikes in front of the building. I was tying my shoes at the time. Squatting near the curb and watching my hands deal with the laces, when I heard the crash and glanced up to see the man and glass. I covered my head thinking they were going to hit me. The glass did. I actually thought that about the man and glass. Things happened so fast. My thought processes, man and glass, screams from the street, screeching car tires whose driver didn't see the glass but thought the man was going to land on his roof. The glass riddled his hood and doors. Some glass landed on my head and clothes. One piece slit my cheek but didn't stay in it, and later a policeman said I should have the cut stitched, but I didn't think it was that bad. He said it'll make a scar if I don't get it stitched, and I said I don't think so and if it's stitched they'll be little scar holes where the needle went in with the thread. I held a handkerchief to my cheek till it was soaked and then someone else's handkerchief till the bleeding stopped. The driver's handkerchief. I offered to give it back or pay for it, but he said it only cost fifty-nine cents plus tax. Then a policeman told him to get his car out of the middle of the street, and I never saw the driver again. The policeman was right. There is a scar. Not one I mind, though. People say it gives me character on what they don't say is a rather bland face. Maybe three people have said it since I got the scar a year ago. One person said "You originally German?" "No." "Not educated there at least?" "No." A total stranger, she spoke to me on a cafeteria line. "It's the scar. I thought you might've gotten it dueling in a German university club." "I didn't think they still did that," I said. "I was in Germany last summer," she said, "Heidelberg, home of the Student Prince, I think, and they definitely do do it, yes."

The man landed on his front and slid a few feet to within a foot of me, his head pointing to my knee. Blood popped out of his nose and mouth some time between the landing and slide, and spattered on my pants and shirt. The glass fell all around us. I yelled "Oh no," and was still. People were screaming. Cars stopped, screeching one first. The whole block seemed to stop, but not all at once. Across the street was a bar with an outdoor patio. The tables were filled and all the people at them seemed to stop. A young woman dressed like a gypsy and leading two unleashed dogs crossing the street stopped, but the dogs started to bark. A troubadour was juggling and standing on a rope strung from a lamppost to a no-parking sign pole in front of the patio. Barefoot, four feet up, one foot raised. Holding three sticks with fire at the ends of them, once he caught the two he'd thrown in the air. The fires didn't stop. He was up there a minute holding the sticks, statuelike, foot raised, staring at the ground, before he jumped down, unfolded an asbestos blanket and wrapped the fire ends of the sticks with it. When he opened it a few seconds later only smoke escaped. A bus at the corner stopped, though I didn't see when, nor when it drove away. I remember hearing a helicopter, but it just went away. And other sounds from far off. Honking. Someone using a machine to get a plaster wall down to the original brick. That never stopped. The man because of the noise his machine made probably didn't hear the window crash or else he didn't want to stop. Later I walked past his window half a block away and saw him using the machine on the wall. Second story also. All the windows open. Furniture covered, mask over his nose, hair plastered white, room nearly stuffed with dust and some of it drifting outside.

Blood ran from the man's face and hands to my knee. He seemed unconscious. I was still holding my shoelaces. I was going to untie and tie the other shoe tight but didn't. I stood up. Movement began on the street again. Both my shoes were still loose, but I wasn't aware of it till I got home. I was going to touch the man to see if he was still breathing but didn't. Cars started up, drove off, people ran over, bus was gone, other people at the tables stood up, the gypsy woman began shrieking and turned around and ran off with her barking dogs. The troubadour made rapid mime looks one after the other: compassion, wonder, confusion, horror, fear, shock, pity, displeasure and then did several mime steps back to the rope and seemed to be concerned, because a woman running to the man on the ground ran into the rope and was choking. He slapped her back, saw she was all right, apologized with his hands and a look, took a lollipop out of her ear and put it into her pocketbook, unhooked the rope from the lamppost, untied the other end from the no-parking sign pole, folded up the rope and put it with his fire-sticks and asbestos blanket into a leather satchel, grabbed his money bag off the sidewalk and tied it to his belt, put his slippers on, satchel over his shoulder and got on a unicycle and made motions with his hands and arms for the people on the sidewalk to clear a path for him and cycled through it and around the corner.

I was so distracted by the actions of the troubadour that for a minute or more I'd forgotten the man on the ground. People had crowded around us. "What happened?" they asked. "Is he okay? Dead? Did he jump? Was he pushed? Is he insane? What caused it, drugs? A fit? Alcohol? Money he owed?" "I don't know," I said, shaking my head, hands over my eyes, on my ears, by my side. "I don't know, I don't know, I don't know."

Later someone said to me "Why did you think he leaped?"

"Did I say he leaped?"

"I heard you. Someone asked how you thought he did it and first you said you didn't know and then that he probably leaped."

"Well, maybe he had to have leaped. If not that then he could only have been thrown out the window headfirst by two very strong men holding an arm and leg of his each, but I don't think that was it. He had to have gotten several feet away from the window and then like a sprinter starting off, ran to it at full speed and leaped. I say that because the window was completely knocked out and it was a big window, almost ceiling to floor, and the old kind, I don't know about the glass, but a thick wooden frame. The mullions as you can see were completely smashed except for a few small pieces hanging to the sides, though not hanging by much. The force of him crashing through the glass, not being pushed, could only have done that, I think. Unless of course four to five very strong men pushed him with all their might from behind at exactly the same time. But then I couldn't explain his dive. No, he leaped."

Several ambulances were called. Before one arrived, someone tried to stop the man's face-bleeding by pressing down on various pressure points, but it didn't work. The man bled a lot. People were horrified: some. A few boys—teenagers—passed by the crowd saying "What happened? What's happening, baby? Hey, look at the stoned-out dude down there," and they all laughed. Some people got angry at the boys but only expressed it to one another or said it aloud to themselves after the boys had left.

An ambulance came. And police and voluntary auxiliary police. The police asked the questions and searched through the second-story apartment and the auxiliary police kept the crowds back and cars from driving along the street. The police asked me the most questions and someone who lived in the man's building, whose answers had to be translated by an auxiliary policewoman, the second most amount of questions. One policeman asked me what did I see? Almost everything. Did you see anyone push him? No. Did you see him jump through the window? No. Did you see anyone else in the apartment before or after he jumped? No. Then what did you see? "I saw him in the air after he leaped through the window."

"How do you know he leaped and wasn't pushed?"

"You said jumped, so I thought you meant leaped, but I don't know if he leaped, jumped or was pushed. Maybe he accidentally fell."

"He didn't. Did he say anything, this man?"

"No."

"On the ground, in the air, from his apartment before he came out?"

"Nothing that I heard."

"What was his expression when he was in the air?"

"He looked like a bird."

"What expression's that?"

"His eyes were open and arms were out and he seemed to have the expression of a flying bird."

"I don't get it. What is that expression? Happiness? Nastiness? Pride in his flying? Hunger, plundering, fear, what?"

"Disconcern."

"You mean unconcern?"

"No concern. No expression. He was just flying. Face like a bird, partially opened beak. Not a calm face like a pigeon but just a face of no concern like a gull or tern."

"To me the gull always looks nasty, and the tern I don't know as a bird."

"The tern looks like a small gull, and the man didn't look nasty, so maybe he didn't look like either of those birds."

"Did he have the expression of someone who you might think had been pushed or thrown out of a window?" No. "You don't live around here then, or not for long?" Wrong. "Where do you live?" I gave my address. Gave my profession. That was when he said he first noticed the slit in my cheek and asked if I'd like the doctor to see it. When I said no, he mentioned the possibility of my getting a scar.

He called over the doctor, who said "Let me see this famous cheek." The doctor applied merthiolate, "just to lessen the chance of getting an infection. If you want that stitched we can have one of the police take you to the hospital too."

"No thanks."

"Getting back to the man," the policeman said. The man was being strapped to a stretcher. He still seemed unconscious. Bandages had been wrapped around his face, hands and neck.

"Excuse me, what?" since we were both watching the stretcher being slid into the ambulance.

"Oh . . . nothing. I don't have any more questions. What's your phone, business or home, so we can reach you?"

I had none but gave him the hours and days I could best be reached at work and home.

"Oh yeah. What, and I don't want to hold you any longer with that cut, were you doing when the man came through the window or seconds before? I have to get that down."

"No problem. Tying my shoes."

"Tying your shoes, good. Though too bad you didn't think of tying them sooner or later."

"Too bad also I wasn't wearing sandals or loafers or those sneakers whatever they're called with no laces which you can just slip on. I was thinking of buying a pair this summer."

"Too bad you didn't."

"Why? I'm not sorry I was here when it happened. Sorry for the man, of course, but not for me. I feel lucky enough I wasn't two feet closer in to the sidewalk, not that I'd ever be, since I always do my shoelace-tying by the curb so people can pass. By the way, what do you think, he'll die?"

"Can't say so but probably no. They usually don't."

The auxiliary police had to clear an opening through the crowd so the ambulance could get through. "Let's go, folks, help them out, help them out," a policeman said, I suppose meaning the ambulance and man inside or the auxiliary police. Lots of people stayed around talking after the ambulance left. Nobody seemed to know the man. "At first I thought I did," someone said, "but then knew I didn't."

"He did live there though," a waiter from the bar patio said, still holding a cocktail tray. "That I'm sure of, as I've seen him coming in and out of that building around the same time at night for five years, though never once in the bar for a drink."

"You've worked here that long, Chuck?" someone said. "I thought for one year, maybe two at the most."

"That long, really. I don't want to sound hackneyed, but it's amazing the way time goes."

"How do you stand it? I heard your boss is a bastard of the worst order."

"Just between you and me and the whole city, he is, but what's not that easy to get these days is a decent living."

"Then you do all right? I wouldn't've thought it."

People passed, stopped, joined the crowd, left, most of those from the beginning or so were gone. Cars were allowed on the street now. The auxiliary police prevented everyone but the tenants from entering the building. Even these people had to show proof, or the landlady, or maybe she was the super sitting on the top step of the stoop, had to give an okay with a head sign or hand wave to the auxiliary police below.

"They'd never let people like that on the real force," someone said, looking at the auxiliary police.

"You mean they're not?" woman behind him said.

"Those four? Your first clue's no gun, which our real cops have to have, on duty or not. They'd also never let them get like what is that big girl there, seventy to eighty pounds overweight, and the tall skinny one in a uniform five times too tight and his hair a pigsty?"

"No gun, that's true. Why do they do it then if they can't even protect themselves?"

"They want to play patrolman, that's why. They're stupid, because they don't even get paid."

"They do a good job," someone else said. "One of them was killed stopping a mugging this year just a few blocks from here."

"That I didn't know. I apologize for all the harsh things I might have said about them."

Suddenly a young man ran up the block screaming "Ricky, Ricky, what's happened to Ricky?"

"Get off that glass," an auxiliary policeman said, holding his club lengthwise across his chest and moving to the man and stepping on the glass himself.

"Glass? Where?" He was right on it. "Oh Christ, I didn't see it. I'll get it in my feet." He jumped around as if the glass was already sticking in him, smashing the glass under his sneakers even more.

"I said get off it, now get off," and the young man ran into the street and around the glass there and tried to get up the building's steps.

"You can't go up there," an auxiliary policewoman said, guarding the steps and holding the club across her chest.

"But my brother Ricky. Somebody said he got hurt. Look at his place."

"He your brother? Excuse me, maybe you should speak to the officer. Officer Gulanus," she yelled to the window.

A policeman stuck his head past the broken window.

"The man's brother he says."

"Come on up here, kid."

The crowd had thinned out by now, but with the appearance of this young man, it grew to the size it was soon after the man had jumped through the window. "The brother," a few people said.

"Of who?" someone said.

"The man who went through that window."

"That what happened? I thought someone got mad at the landlord there and busted it out. The guy die?"

"From one story up ten feet to the ground? He more likely only got a sprained ankle and walked away."

"That's his brother all right," the waiter said, coming over again, this time with no tray. "I've seen him around too. Mostly helping his brother up the stairs when his brother was dead drunk or high on drugs. I couldn't tell which."

"You should speak to the policeman there," I said.

"Why?"

"I don't know. Maybe what you said could be useful."

"I got work to do and my own reasons for not talking to police."

"What a neighborhood," someone said to me.

"It has its moments."

"Moments hell. You live around here?"

"Few blocks away."

"How could you? There's craziness all around every minute of the day. Pimps, whores, cars running you over, burglars, pickpockets, muggers, women getting raped, drunks, bums, people peddling dollar joints right under your nose, three card monte sharks right nearby cheating everyone blind with their shills. I'm from Chicago and we're supposed to be bad, right? Riots, gangsters, politicians who fraud your votes and install their friends, but we're not a quarter to what you guys are. You've a family to live with too?"

"No."

"I was thinking if you had one and lived here, I'd really feel sorry for you. I don't mean to be rude, but if I was told I had to on my life raise my little kids in this neighborhood, and we just have one, I'd kill them both."

"Okay, show's over, why not everyone go home?" an auxiliary policeman said.

"Because it's a slow Tuesday night," someone said. This made a few people laugh.

"Listen to them," the man said to me. "People would never speak to a cop like that in Chicago. They'd be considerate, would listen to what he said, or be afraid of getting their head bashed in by one."

"It's only meaningless talk," I said. "No harm to it."

"That's what you have to think perhaps, but you're going to see one happy guy to leave this hole tomorrow," and he moved on.

By now I could only recognize two people from the original crowd, and the landlady and auxiliary and regular police. In the window I could see the young man crying and the policeman with his arm around the boy's shoulder.

"Is that the kid who jumped?" someone said. "He looks okay to me."

"He's standing at least," someone else said. "That's a lot more than you can say for a lot of people in this area."

I wanted to say something to correct their information or interpretation of the situation and even of this neighborhood, but didn't. It was already an hour since the man had jumped or whatever he'd done through that window. The waiter was going off-duty for the night. At least I assumed so because he had his street clothes on and was heading for the avenue, but maybe he was only on his break. The policeman got in a patrol car with the young man. The auxiliary police continued to guard the glass part of the sidewalk and the building stoop.

"What are they going to do, arrest the kid for breaking a window?" someone said, watching the patrol car drive away.

"If they do, don't worry, tomorrow he'll be out bright and early to break another window or somebody's leg," someone else said.

I started to walk out of the crowd.

"He wasn't the one who jumped, was he?" someone said, meaning me.

"I think so. He's got the blood all over his clothes, and did you see his face?"

"Not him," a third person said. "He was standing on the sidewalk when the lady on the stoop there threw a TV set out of the window."

"Was she throwing it at him?"

"Go ask him. All I know is she threw it out without first opening the window, and whether it's the glass or TV that hit him is a good guess. Somebody did say a man grabbed the TV right after it landed and ran away with it."

"When it was so smashed up?"

"Apparently it wasn't."

A few blocks away the troubadour from before had drawn a chalk circle with a diameter of maybe twenty feet on a sidewalk corner. A crowd was standing on the outside perimeter of the circle two and three deep. I stood and watched his act for a while. He rode the unicycle on the circle lines a few times, never once getting more than half an inch off the line either way. While he was riding he took a hat off a woman's head and put it on a man's head a few feet away. He tried to light someone's cigarette while he was riding but couldn't do it after three tries, and snatched the cigarette out of the man's mouth on the fourth time around and threw it away. He did manage to take a watch off a woman's wrist while he was riding, and gave it back to her his next time around when she didn't even know it was gone. Then he put the bike on its side and did tricks with his hat, rolling it down his arms and catching it just before it touched the ground, balancing it on his nose, knee and toes and kicking it off his toes and landing it on his head. He next did a juggling act with scissors, hatchets and knives and then the same juggling act with a borrowed kerchief around his mouth, which broke most people up, and then with the kerchief tied around his eyes, which got the most applause. He gave the kerchief back to the woman, looked angry at her and took a gun out of his hat. Someone screamed and he swiveled around and aimed the gun at the screamer and pulled the trigger and out flew a parachute with a message attached to it at the ends of the strings which said "These days, generosity really counts." Then he bowed and passed the hat around. He did quite well. Got lots of compliments also. One woman said to him she'd traveled throughout Europe and Eurasia and had never seen a performer with so many consummate skills. A man emptied his change purse into the hat and said "Bravo, Horatio, you are simply divine, the world's best." When the troubadour shoved the hat in front of me, I backed away and nearly fell off the curb. Someone grabbed my arm to stop me from falling. At that moment when this person was helping me to stand straight again, the crowd was laughing. When I turned around, the troubadour's painted white face was right up against mine and he suddenly jumped back and shook his body and head as if I'd just frightened him. Then he continued to pass the hat around and I walked home.

Arrangements

She comes into my room. I hold her hand. She kisses my lips. We undress one another and go to bed. Later, she dresses and leaves. I sleep for a little while and dress and go outside. I see her talking to a man on the street. I say "Hey, how are you?"

"Excuse me," she says, "but I don't think we've met."

"Harry. Harry Lipton."

"Harry Lipton? No, the name's not familiar either."

"Harry Trusky then."

"Trusky? No, try again."

"Harry Bittom."

"Bittom, Bittom. Now that's much less better. I'm sorry." She turns her back to me and resumes talking to the man. He looks at me over her shoulder.

"How do you do?" he says.

"Hello." I put out my hand. We shake.

"Arnold Peters," he says.

"Harry Fortundale."

"Fortundale," he says. "How's it going today?"

"Fine. Couldn't be better." Her back is still turned to me. "Do you think you can introduce us?" I say to him.

"You mean you and the lady?"

"The lady and I, yes."

"What was your name again?"

"Harry Levitt."

"Harry Levitt, Gretchen Morley. Gretchen Morley, Harry Levitt."

She turns to me, puts out her hand. We shake. She says "Nice to meet you. What do you do?"

"Lots of things," I say. "Work, sleep, eat."

"And make jokes too, I bet."

"Make jokes, don't make jokes. Run, walk, play, read, dream."

"And change your name whenever you want to?"

"Change my name, don't change my name. Dress, undress, make my bed, cook."

"And have women up to your room, I bet."

"Have women up to my room, don't have women there. Tie my shoelaces, don't. Buy clothes, give them away. Things. Many things."

"And kiss and make love, I bet."

"Kiss, make love, don't. Sometimes. Sometimes it seems like never. Turn on and off lights. You know. What do you do?"

"All of those except the name change. Talk to people mostly. I like talking to people best."

"I don't," Arnold says, walking away.

"He makes jokes too," she says. "Wait up, Arnold," she yells at him.

But he's turned the corner, is gone.

"Now it's just us two," she says.

"If you mean together here, yes."

"What would you like to do?"

"Talk. Go up to my room with you. Talk to you there. I find you very attractive."

"That's all?"

"Interesting, intelligent, sensitive, warm."

"I mean, that's all you want to do in your room?"

"Undress you, be undressed by you."

"That's all?"

"Have you come in my room after I'm already in my room and on my bed, and then get in my bed."

"That's all?"

"To make love, why not?"

"Where do you live?"

"Sixth brownstone up the street, north side, top floor, apartment C."

"I'll be there," she says.

"How long will it take?"

"Does that depend on both of us or do you mean how long you want it to take me to get to your room?"

"Leave here two minutes after I've gone. That will give me time."

"To do what?"

"Get to my building, up the stairs, unlock the door, go in, close the door, make my bed, peel an orange, set it out on the night table for us to eat and lie on my bed."

"I don't like oranges. No citrus. Too acidy. And just before one gets into bed, too sticky to eat."

"Then just to make my bed."

"It's not necessary. Except if you want to put on fresh linen, that's okay with me."

"Then give me five minutes after I leave."

"Five minutes from . . . now."

I run to my building, up the stairs, unlock my door, into my apartment, close the door, take the linens off the bed and throw them in the closet, get fresh linens out of the dresser and put them on the bed, peel an orange, eat it, wash my hands and lips and dry them, and just as I hear her footsteps on the last flight of stairs, dump the peels and pits into the garbage bag and jump on the bed.

She comes into the room. I hold her hand.

"We didn't say anything about your holding my hand," she says.

I drop her hand.

"We also didn't say anything about your dropping my hand."

"I didn't know what else to do with it. All I could think of doing with the hand I held were several other things we hadn't arranged to do. So I thought the next best thing to my not having done something we hadn't arranged to do was to stop doing what we hadn't arranged to do, which couldn't have been to continue holding your hand."

"We also hadn't arranged to confuse one another." She kisses my lips.

"We didn't say anything before about your kissing my lips," I say.

"Do you mind?"

"Nor anything about asking if I minded or not once you did something we hadn't arranged to do."

"What do you want me to do, unkiss you?"

"Let's just say we're even now. Both of us having done something to the other that we hadn't arranged to do and then doing our best to undo it."

We undress one another and she gets into bed. We make love. Later, she begins dressing.

"We didn't say anything about your dressing," I say.

"If I'm to leave, one of us has to dress me. Since we didn't arrange that either, I decided to dress myself."

"We also hadn't arranged your leaving here."

"Neither my staying nor you."

"Then how do we undo now what we didn't arrange to do?"

"By your dressing and leaving with me or soon after me. Then we'd be on the street where we first started arranging things, which would make us even again I suppose, though I haven't quite figured that one out yet."

"We didn't say anything about figuring things out either. Better, why don't you undress and come back to bed? We did arrange that."

"We arranged you undressing me and my coming to bed, but we didn't say how many times. Why don't we forget whatever arrangements we made and from now on do only what we want to or have to do?"

"But we didn't arrange forgetting our arrangements or really forgetting anything."

"We arranged to talk, right? So now we're talking about forgetting our arrangements."

"Let me think about it. I realize we didn't arrange anything about my thinking about it, though I also know that everything we do together or apart can't be arranged. All right. We'll make a new arrangement to make no more arrangements. You think it could work?"

"We'll see, darling, we'll see."

I get out of bed, take her hand and help undress her. We get back into bed. We stay there for two days. In bed. Occasionally out of bed, but never out of the room. Cooking, cleaning, washing, eating. Sleeping together, making love. Dressing, undressing, each other and ourselves. Reading. Doing many things we hadn't arranged to do and some things we never did together or apart. Most of it works. My cooking and her cleaning doesn't too well, but we agree they can be improved. We don't tire of one another after two days. That's something we never could have known. We laugh more. We have more fun, cry a few times over past memories and present happiness, hold each other more too. Then she says "Let's go out."

"I don't know if I want to."

"That's all right. But I do, so I'm going out, with or without you."

"Sure. You're right. Who says no? But suddenly I want to go out too, more with you than without you. Much more."

We dress ourselves. I hand her her coat. She finds my scarf and wraps it around my neck. We go out. We see Arnold Peters walking on the street. He says "Hello you two, how's it going?"

"Can't complain," she says. "As for Harry, he'll have to speak for himself."

"Harry, that's right," he says. "What was your last name again?"

"Raskin."

"I'm sorry, I didn't get that."

"Raskin. Harry Raskin."

"Big change over this guy," he says to her. "How you been, Harry?"

"Fine. Couldn't be better. You?"

"Not so good."

"Too bad. Anything I can do for you?"

"You can give her some time to let me take her out for a night."

"I think that's her decision."

"You're damn right it's my decision," she says. "Sorry, Arnold, but no."

"Tough luck," he says. "It would have been fun for me at least." He goes.

"I don't like him anymore," she says. "And won't, unless he changes."

We go to her hotel, tell the night clerk she's checking out, pack her things and carry them to my apartment. She's moved in. We share many things: dresser, bed, bathroom glass, expenses. We both cook, work, clean the apartment. She has a child. We get married. We move several times, but always stay together. Occasionally she takes a business trip or vacation on her own or with the child and occasionally I do the same. Sometimes we all go together. A few times we leave our son with a nurse and each of us goes off separately on business trips or vacations and stay away for the same or different lengths of time. When our son gets old enough to stay home alone for a while, we go off together or separately, on business trips or vacations and sometimes we all go off separately or together, and sometimes just one of us with our son or she and I together while the other stays home or takes a vacation or business trip alone. Then our son moves out. We get a smaller apartment. We divorce but come back together again after a few years but don't remarry. By this time our son is living with a woman and they have a child. We get old. One day she gets quite sick. Her temperature stays high for two days. The doctor comes and says she has to be moved to a hospital immediately, it's that serious. I sit beside her while we wait for the ambulance to come. I hold her hand.

She says "We didn't say anything about your holding my hand."

"Are you delirous?" I say.

"Yes."

"I know what you mean now. I forgot. No, we didn't say anything about my holding your hand. But I thought you might want me to. I know I wanted to. And it feels good, doesn't it?"

She nods, closes her eyes, dies.

I go off, but it's never the same with anyone else after that.

Guests

Come in. Over here. Sit down. Make yourself at home. Are you comfortable? Like something to drink? To eat? I want to tell you something. How about another cushion? Different seat? Try the couch. It's much more comfortable. The other side—that one has bad springs. Push away the cat. Then I'll get him away. Rosy, get off. I said to get off. There. You're allergic to cat hair? By the way you sneezed. Maybe you don't know you are. Rosy, get out of the room. He never listens. Off the chair yes but not out of the room. And she I mean. To me all cats are hes, isn't that ridiculous? Particularly if you caught two copulating. Because to most people cats are shes. Which would be just as ridiculous if you caught them in the act. But not to me. I mean to me all dogs are shes. But I'll get her out of the room just in case you are allergic. Some people only become that way to cats later in life. When they're adults like you and I. Or like you and me. I can almost never get those two straight too. Rosy, come here. Thataboy. To me she'll always be a boy. I'll throw him out of the room and close the door. There. Now watch. You probably won't sneeze again or at least not for the time you're here.

Now about what I have to tell you. I haven't forgotten. But you sure you don't need more cushions? One more then. It's

only on the other chair. I'll get it. No bother. Put it behind
your back. Then in top of the couch where your head or neck
can rest. How does it feel? Much better I bet. And notice you're
not sneezing anymore. I told you it was the cat. What's that?
Another sneeze? It could be from the newspaper ink. So you've
never sneezed from it that you know. Though I always say it's
what you don't know that counts. I don't always say it but have
thought of it often and occasionally said it I believe. At least a
few times. Maybe only once. Could be I only just thought of it
before and once. But I'll take the newspaper away and throw it
into the other room with the cat. Let's see if he sneezes from
the ink. If you sneeze again with both of them out of the room,
I'll almost believe you're allergic to me.

So what I want to talk to you about. It's quite important.
Very. Though like some music on first? Simple for me to do.
Mozart or Bach? To me they're the only true composers. Plus a
couple of others—Beethoven of course. And Handel and Haydn,
Vivaldi and Bartok. Which would you like? Also Stravinsky,
Gabrieli, Mahler and Pärt. Let me also get you that drink. It
doesn't have to be stronger than iced tea. Or any mix you want
that goes with gin except grapefruit juice I've got. Okay, one
coming up. I'll also select what music to play if you won't. Now
what do you think? About the drink and this piece. His number
twenty-four. For piano and orchestra. Guess which composer.
Wrong. Guess again. Again wrong. I hate guessing games and
often the people who participate in them. It's not, though,
Mozart.

Where was I again? What I wanted to tell you. Have to.
Important. Extremely. Almost more than I can say. We're both
comfortable though, correct? Drink. Music. Volume not too loud
or low. Reasonably soft couch on that side and mine a relatively
easy seat. Air. How's the air? I can turn the air conditioner down
or off. I'll leave it at medium. I only had it at high to quickly
cool the room, not that it's that muggy out or hot. But you get

used to these things. I do, I don't know about you. Maybe you
don't even own one. I almost keep it on steadily till people tell
me there's a cold wave out. Almost not true. A minor exagger-
ation. But I think I do overabuse this machine and help create
a minor energy crisis with it all by myself. At least for this city.
But enough of me and our city. Let's get down to what I brought
you here to tell you. Because you're quite comfortable now,
right? Pleasant temperature in the room. Pleasant room. It is a
pleasant room, isn't it? Designed the entire place myself. Rebuilt
the walls and mixed the paints to get that color which I'm
wondering if you find too bright or even like. And the lights?
They also too bright? I can turn them down. Turn them off
even, which wouldn't be too smart to do, though we'd still have
the little light from the stereo. At least sufficient light from it to
find the wall switch. Furniture's all mine too, built from scratch.
From wood, actually, but you knew what I meant. Everyone's
allowed a little joke, even before the crematorium. So here we
are. Pleasant temperature and room, agreed? And I hope you
know that was a statement about the joke in general and not a
joke about the crematorium. Cool drink in your hand. Like a
refill? I won't go around calling you a heavy drinker. I usually
like a quick one myself and then to linger over the second for
half an hour or more. Though linger over your second, if you
have one, for fifteen minutes or ten or even five if you like. Or
finish your first, knock down the second and linger over a third.
Whatever you wish. While you're here, my home is yours. I'll
get you that refill. No bother. There. Cool drink again. Music—
too loud or do you even like this piece? I'll change it if you
want. To viola, solo piano, anything with voice or strings. Something more modern or jazzier, I have those too. Fine. Music.
Room. Temperature and drink. Pleasant everything. Best part
of the couch. Cat and newspaper out of the room. And you're
still not sneezing anymore. So I suppose it was the newspaper

you were allergic to, if you don't sneeze here again, or a delayed end of allergic reaction to the cat.

But what I practically had to drag you here to tell you about. That's what I now have to speak to you about. That's what I think is foremost in my mind. It is. I don't just think so but know. Unbelievably important. But come in. Sit down. Over here. Make yourself comfortable. You are comfortable. You are here and sitting in this room. All that's true. In the best seat in the house. And I'm sitting here lingering over a drink and being comfortable across from you. Anyway, what was it again I had to talk to you about? Suddenly I forgot. I'm sure I can remember it if I try. Let me think. I'm trying. I can't remember. No bother. Drink up and if you don't want another and I can't remember before you leave what I wanted so urgently to tell you, I know we can save it for another time.

Gifts

I wrote a novel for Sarah and sent it to her. She wrote back "For me? How sweet. Nobody has ever done anything or presented me with anything near to what you've just given me. I'll treasure it always. I must confess I might not get around to reading it immediately, since I am tied up to my neck and beyond with things I'm forced to do first. But I can't describe my pleasure in receiving this and the overwhelming gratitude I'll always have in knowing it was written especially for me."

I painted a series of paintings and crated and shipped them to her and she wrote back "Are these really all for me? I only looked in one of them and it said '1st of a series of 15,' and I counted the other crates and came up with fourteen more and thought 'My God, I have the entire series.' You can't imagine how this gift moves me. I'll open the rest of the crates as soon as I find the time, as I have been unrelievedly busy these past few days and will be for weeks. The one I did open I'll hang above my fireplace if I can find the space among my other paintings and prints. Meanwhile, it's safely tucked away in a closet, so don't fear it will get hurt. Again, what can I say but my eternal thanks."

I wrote a sonata for her and called it "The Sarah Piece" and had it printed and sent her a copy and she wrote me "A musical composition in my name? And for the one instrument I can play if not competently then at least semipublically okay? You've gone out of your way to honor and please me more than anyone has and a lot more than any person should expect another to for whatever the reasons, and as soon as I can sever myself from all the other things I'm doing and which I wish I had the time to tell you about, I'll sit down and try to learn this sonata or at least read it through. You can't believe the many good things that have happened to me lately and which I'm so involved in, but I'll definitely find the time to attend to my sonata in one of the ways I mentioned, of that you can bet. Once more my warmest thanks for your thoughtfulness and my respects for your creativeness, and my very best.''

I carved sculptures for her, designed and built furniture for her, potted and baked earthenware for her, wrote poems, plays and essays for her and after I completed each of these projects I sent it to her and her replies were usually the same. Her thanks. I could never know how much it means to her. She is continually amazed by the diversity of my talents and skills. She will read, look at or use this newest thing as soon as she can. Then, after I sent her a coverlet I wove and thought good enough to use as a wall hanging and maybe the best thing I'd ever made, she wrote ''You've sent me so many things that I don't know what to open or look at or hang or put in its rightful place or eat off of first. And not wanting to give any of your creative forms preference over the others, I'm going to set aside one of the dozen rooms here for your work and call that room the Arthur T. Reece Retreat in honor of you and put all your gifts in it so I know that whenever I want to go through any of these works or have found a place in one of the other rooms to put one of them or even when I want to think of you creating and making all these things for me, I can enter that room. The room, by the way, has no windows. It does have a wash basin and door but with no lock on it. It is a small room, once the maid's quarters of the previous owners, so most of the things you sent me will have to be piled on top of one another, though know that'll be done extra carefully. I am having the door taken off and the space it makes bricked up. I am cutting that room off from the rest of the house. I am going to set that separated room afire in honor of the great passion you've put into your work and your obvious deep feelings for me. I am honored, I am grateful, I am amazed and touched and of course ever thankful and moved, I have never known anyone more creative and generous than you. No, I am joking. I have given away all your gifts from the start and have told the post office and other delivery services to turn back any further envelope, package or crate coming from you. No, I am joking. I am disassociating myself from all the other men I know and whatever activities I'm now involved in and want you to come live with me immediately as loving soulmates and man, parents and wife. No, I am joking. I never received any of the things you claimed to friends you sent me and am beginning to doubt they all could have gotten lost along the way. No, I am joking. They all arrived but I quickly turned them into refuse. Aside from that, I am happily married, with child for the first time in my life, and wonder why you think you know me well enough to keep sending these things to me without my eventually getting disturbed and insulted by them and where you initially got my address and name. No, I am joking. I appreciate all you've done, have enjoyed the attention and sold whatever I could of these gifts for whatever I could get for them and with that money I am about to embark on a trip around the world with my newest lover who is also my best friend and one of our finest progressive artists. No, I am joking. It was nice of you to make all these things for me but I'm sorry to say, almost ashamed to after all I've said in my previous letters and just put you through, that I wasn't once, and this is the absolute truth now, impressed. When one has it one has it and you've proven over and over again that you never had it and so will never have it so why bother trying anything out again in any field or form or at least on me? You do and whatever it is you send me I shall throw up on before returning it to you cash on delivery in its envelope, box or crate."

I sent her a silver necklace someone else made but in my cover letter to her I said I fashioned it with my own homemade tools. She wrote back "For the first time, and I'm as serious now as I was at the end of my last letter, I love what you've made for me and think you've adopted a creative form that suits you perfectly and which you serve extraordinarily well. Good luck and success with it and much thanks." I sent her more of this person's jewelry and after the first few packages each one came back with a post office message stamped on it saying address unknown. I still send jewelry to her and other things I buy or sometimes find but say I made and they always come back. The few friends I know who know her say they also don't know where she's gone. The post office is right, they say. "Despite how much we all adored her and thought the feeling was mutual if not more so from her to some of us, she told no one she was going and left no forwarding address."

In Time

I'm walking along a street when a woman from a building nearby yells "Help, save me, they're trying to kill me in here right now." I look up. She's waving to me from a window on the fourth floor. Then it seems she's being pulled into the room by her feet, holds onto the sill a couple of seconds, is pulled all the way in and the window closes, shade drops. I look for a short while more but there's no further activity from there.

It's evening, around nine, beginning of summer so still a little light. Nobody else is on the street or looking out of any of the windows on the block. Couple cars come. I run into the street to stop them to get some help for the woman. First car passes me before I get there and second swerves around me, driver sticking his fist out the window and cursing me, and at the corner both cars go through a red light.

I look back at that building. Shade and window are still down. I look around for a phone booth. There's none on this street and all the stores and businesses are locked up for the night if not the weekend. I could walk several blocks to the main avenue and try to get help there, or call the police from one of the public phones that could be along the way. But the woman's in immediate danger it seems, so I go into the building to do what I can for her without getting hurt myself.

There are ten buttons on the bell plate and I ring all of them. Nobody answers. Most are businesses. Arbuckle Ltd this, Tandy & Son that, except for a nameless bell on the fifth floor and Mrs. Ivy Addison in 4F. That has to be her: fourth floor front. I ring her bell several more times. If anything is happening to her, maybe this will distract the person doing it.

I yell through the door "Someone, come down or ring me in, a woman in your building's in trouble." No response and I try the door. It's open. I go outside, look up at her window. Everything's the same there and there are no cars or people on the street or lights on in any of the building's windows. I go through the vestibule, hesitate on the bottom steps, say to myself "You've got to go up and try to help, you wouldn't be the same after if you just left here," and walk upstairs, knocking on all the doors I pass till I reach the fourth floor.

There are two doors at opposite ends of the hallway: 4F and 4R. I knock on 4F, step back to the stairs, ready to run down them. No one comes to the door. I ring the bell this time and knock, get back to the stairs, even a couple of steps down them. Nobody answers. Then I hear the vestibule door close and someone coming upstairs. I look down the stairwell. The hand on the banister seems to belong to a woman. She passes the first flight and is walking up the second.

"Hello?" I yell down the well.

"Yes, you speaking to me?"

"Do you know who lives in 4F? Because before when I was on the street—"

"Excuse me, just a second, I don't hear too good: my ears. Wait till I get to your floor."

She walks up the second flight, around the landing and is now at the bottom of the stairs I'm on. An older woman, around seventy, old clothes, hearing aid, holding onto the banister for support, limping upstairs. "Now what is it you want to know?"

"You see before, I was on the street, few minutes ago at the most, when I heard this woman in 4F here yelling 'Help, save me—' "

"Oh her. She always does that. You must be new in this neighborhood."

"I don't live in this neighborhood. I was just taking a walk."

"A walk around here?" She's two steps from me now. I get against the wall so she can pass. She stops. "Why would you want to take a walk in this neighborhood? There's nothing to see or do once the stores and factories close for the day and they been closed for three hours. She's the only excitement we got on the block, and her racket like she screamed to you almost every day. 'Help save me' my eye. She's crazy, you know."

"No I didn't."

"Crazy as bedbugs. Ever see a bedbug?"

"No."

"Neither have I. My homes, even as a kid, poor as we were then and am, have always been spotless clean, though I bet hers haven't. But that's the expression they use. Bedbugs must be crazy or move in a crazy motion, wouldn't you say?"

"I think that's it. They sort of dart round and round when the covers are suddenly thrown off them or lights go on, or maybe that's only roaches. Anyway, if she's that crazy, I guess I better be going. False alarm as they say."

"False what?"

"Alarm. An old expression also. Like a fire. Someone puts an alarm in, firemen come—"

"Oh yeah, I remember. Okay, nice talking to you."

I start to walk downstairs. She steps in my way. Door opens above me. 4F, where the crazy woman is. I turn to look. Another older woman, looking much like this one, same features, same kind of old clothes, though one on the stairs has on a coat and hat.

"Hello there," woman above me says.

I look back at the woman on the stairs thinking 4F's talking to her, but she says "I think she's speaking to you, dear."

"Me?"

"Hello there," 4F says. "Won't you come in and help me, save me. I'm quite calm now."

"Why don't you?" woman on the stairs says. "She's very nice. Give you a good cup of coffee or tea if you prefer and interesting talk. I know. I've heard it over and over again till my head aches."

"No thanks," I say, and then trying to pass her: "Excuse me."

"Where you think you're going?"

"Outside for sure."

"Oh, you must be crazy as bedbugs also to think you can. You go straight upstairs, dear. Me and my sister have great plans for you."

"The hell you do," and I push past her. She hooks her foot around my ankle. I try catching myself but can't and as I start falling downstairs she shoves me hard from behind and I fly over a few steps, stick out my hands and land on them and slide the rest of the way down, my head bumping on every step. I lie there awhile, whole body hurting, head and hands bleeding, several of my teeth out and lips split I think, and then try standing.

"You coming quietly or need help, dear?" she says above me.

"No, I got to go," and make it to one knee.

"Last time," and I say "I already told you," and she comes down on my head with something like a stone a few times and I drop to the ground.

Next thing I know they're carrying me into an apartment. Next thing after that I'm sitting on a couch, arms and legs bound, head wrapped with a bandage, the two women washing my hand wounds. The one who yelled out the window to me says "Listen, why you giving us such a big fuss? We just want you to hear our little story, and then if you're a good boy and hear it all without squawking, we'll let you go. Now here's two aspirins to take care of the pain that must be in your head and mouth."

She puts them on my tongue and her sister gives me some water to swallow them and after a few minutes of watching them bandage my hands I fall asleep.

They don't tell me any stories or let me go. They just keep me there and go about their regular routine it seems, shopping and cooking, ironing and cleaning, embroidering and watching TV, when they're not taking care of my needs.

They give me their bedroom and I'm always bound in ropes, even when I sleep, usually my arms and legs both, and carried to the various places I have to be carried to to eat, bathe, sit, rest, go to the toilet and other things. At first I shout and complain a lot about my predicament, calling them crazies, harpies, sadists, and they say "Don't use such ugly words around the house," and slap my face and hands and gag me and a couple of times wash my mouth out with soap. I shout and complain much less over the next few weeks because the slaps and gags hurt and the soap tastes awful, but every so often I have to let it out of me and I get more of the same.

They never talk to me or treat me like an adult. "Want some more foodie, Charles?" they say and I either nod or shake my head. If I shake my head they still put the food on a spoon and jam it against my lips till I open them and eat the food. Once a week they sit me in a bathtub with my arms and legs tied and bathe and shampoo me. "Close your eyes or they'll burn," they say, and I do because if I don't they'll let the suds run into my eyes till they burn.

Otherwise they mostly ignore me. They turn the TV on and we all watch it or just I watch it while they put away groceries or read or play cards. If they talk about the TV show or what they read in the newspapers that day, they never include me in the conversation. When I try to get in it, just to talk to someone as an adult and maybe pass the time faster, they say things like "You know the old adage, Charles: Children should be seen and not . . . what?" If I don't answer them they say "And not what, Charles, and not what?" and hold their hands above my face ready to slap it and I say "And not heard," and they smile and pat my head. If I still try to get in their conversation they always slap and gag me.

Once a week or so I ask "When will you tell me your story so I can go?" and they say "Be still."

"Then when will you just let me go?" and they say "In time, dear."

"How long is that?" and they say "In time means in time, now you want the gag or to get slapped or maybe both?"

If I then say "Then just tell me what the hell you're keeping me here for," they say "Now watch your tongue, Charles, or you really will get gagged and slapped and maybe more."

Twice I yelled after they said that "Okay, slap me, gag me you old crabs, you hags, you crazies, you homicides," and they ran over to me and shoved the gag into my mouth and slapped my face and pulled my hair and knocked me off the chair and kicked me in the chest and head and then carried me to my bed and said "You'll be let out and fed when you get to have better manners to people in general and respect for your elders in particular, which might be only one of the reasons we brought you here," and locked the door and didn't open it till around the same time next day.

If I could escape I would. But my bedroom window has a double gate on it and in all the times I've tried I've never once freed my arms or legs from the ropes. After three months of this I say to them "I can't stand it anymore. Either you release me immediately or I'm going on a hunger strike till you let me go."

"All right," they say. "Cut your nose off to spite your you-know-what," and carry me to bed and leave me alone there for three days without anything to eat, drink or listen to and nothing to look at but the ceiling, walls and window shade. I get so hungry, thirsty, dirty and bored that I shout "Ivy and Roz?" They come in and Roz says "No false alarms?" and I say "None. From now on I'll be a good little boy and eat and drink regularly and won't ask again when I'm leaving here." They pat my head, clean and feed me and sit me in front of the TV, but only to programs they want.

A few times I plead with them to give me some physical work to do. "Anything, even for eight to ten hours a day straight without pay. Just to do something to get my body back in shape and spend my time some other way but watching television and wasting away here."

"If we free your arms or legs you might swing at us or gallop out of here," and I say "Then give me something mentally stimulating to do, like a crossword puzzle to look at and work out in my head or a newspaper or a book with words in it on pages which I can turn with my nose."

"Concentrate on improving your personality and conduct further. Because for someone of your incorrigible willfulness and stubbornness, that'll be work and time spent well enough."

"Please, you've got to, I'm going nuts here," and they say "Want to go on another hunger strike though this one organized by us?" and I shut up.

It takes a few months more before I do everything they say or what I figure they want me to, except every third week or so when I have to scream out my frustrations about staying here and having nothing to do, and then I get gagged and slapped and strapped to my bed without food and water for a day.

Fall goes, then winter and spring, then summer and fall again, seasons, years. Because my behavior's tremendously improved they say, once a month I'm allowed to sit by the living room window for an hour during the day and look through a slit in the blinds to the street. It ends up being the event I look forward to most in my life, other than getting out of here. I watch the old buildings being renovated and pray that the owner of this one sells the building and it gets gutted and renovated too. I watch the styles of cars and clothes change, new tenants move in, old ones move out, neighborhood kids get taller and fuller and rowdier year after year.

While I sit behind that slit I often crave that someone will notice my eyes somehow—maybe through a roaming pair of binoculars or just from above average eyesight—and discover that I'm almost constantly blinking the S.O.S. signal with my lids for the hour a month I'm there. Or maybe someone will think how odd it is that once a month only, a pair of twitching eyes looks onto the street for an hour, at least odd enough to wonder about it to the point of perhaps one of these months phoning the police to check out this apartment.

The only outsider who ever comes to the apartment is the building's super, who every other year or so is called in to fix a pipe or light switch. When that happens I'm gagged, strapped to the bed and locked in my room and the super comes and fixes whatever's the matter without knowing I'm here.

Once, two years ago, someone else did ring the bell. It was the only other live-in tenant in the building, the nameless one from the fifth floor. I was quickly gagged but overheard her say through the door that she was going out of town for a week to a funeral, so if Ivy or Roz hear anyone lurking around upstairs late in the evening, to call the police. "Will do," Roz said and the woman said "Thank you and have a good week," and that as far as I know was the last time she came by.

After being here for several years I long for something like a tornado to sweep through this part of the city and destroy every building in its path, though without anyone getting hurt except Ivy and Roz, but especially this building. Or that only this one catch fire somehow, when the factories are closed and the nameless tenant's out, but really anytime if it has to come to that, just to give me some small chance of getting away or being found alive.

I hope for a disaster like one of those for about a year and then decide to make one of my own. Twice a year on their birthdays they put a candle on the dinner table and the sister whose birthday it is blows it out at the end of the meal. I make my plans during Ivy's birthday dinner, rehearse it to myself day after day. When Roz's birthday comes several months later and they're in the kitchen preparing a special dessert and I'm sitting at the table with my arms and legs tied, I manage to stand and roll my body across the table and knock the candle to the floor. The rug starts to burn, just as I intended it to, and I get on my knees and blow on the fire to make it spread. The sisters smell the burning rug, run in, douse the fire with water before it becomes anything more than a small blaze, then gag me, light the candle and hold my hand over it till my skin sizzles and the gag almost pops from my soundless screams.

"That'll teach you never to play with fire or spoil my party for Roz," Ivy says and they take the gag off and I tell them I won't try any tricks like that again.

"You do and you'll get worse, much worse, maybe twice as many years with us than we planned for you," and I say "I promise, never again."

That's the first definite hint that my stay here won't be forever, unless they're lying. But it does get my hopes up somewhat that I'll be released eventually and I don't question them on it or make any trouble in the next three years. I become the model prisoner: courteous, obedient, uncomplaining, silent except to their questions and demands, always responding how they want me to and keeping out of their way. In that time I grow bald, my skin and body hairs turn gray, muscles continue to atrophy, I get so thin and weak from no exercise and their inadequate food that I can no longer turn myself over in bed, and my teeth ache night and day from my years of untreated cavities here, which they don't give me anything for but two aspirins a week.

Then, eight years to the day I got here, they take my ropes off after dinner and say "All right, you can go." I say "Thanks," not believing they mean it, and sit there at the table, taking my pleasure in being free of the ropes for the first time in eight years and wondering how many minutes it'll be before they're put back on.

"What are you waiting for," Roz says, "another eight years? You'll get it, though we sure as shoot don't want you around for that long again, if you don't move your behind out of here now."

Maybe they're not kidding, and I try to stand but am so unused to it this way that I drop back in the chair and it falls over with me to the floor. They help me up and say "This is the way to do it: spread your legs apart—rest—then one step after the next—rest . . . you'll get the knack back in time," and walk me to the door.

"My things," I say. "What I came here with and probably all I got left in the world," and Roz says "If you mean your wallet, watch and ring and stuff, all those are partial but final payment for your room, board and care these years. You're getting off cheap, Charles," and they push me a few inches past the threshold and shut and lock the door.

I still think they're playing with me and will suddenly throw open the door, knock me to the ground and carry me back inside. I only begin to believe I'm really free from them when I reach the bottom landing and open the vestibule door.

"Fresh air," I say. "The moon and stars—they're really there." My legs get wobbly and I sit on their building's stoop and take lots of deep breaths and then stay there because all my energy got used up making my way downstairs. It's almost dark, about the time of night when I was first on this block nobody on the street or at the windows, no passing cars. "People—help me,"

I want to shout, but my voice is too weak for even the next door first-floor tenant to hear.

Someone must have seen me and phoned the police—maybe even the sisters—because a squad car comes especially for me a half-hour later. I put my arms out to him and he says "Too much to drink tonight, eh pal?"

"Not it at all. I've been kidnapped by two sisters in this building for the last eight years and was only just now released."

"Eight you say. Good story. Why not ten years?—let's go for twelve. At least yours is a little better story than the next wino's, though you're in a lot worse shape than most," and calls for an ambulance.

In the hospital I tell the police I'm no drunk and never was. "The doctors can vouch there's not a drop of alcohol in my blood or on my breath, and if you phone my best friend, if he's still alive, he'll tell you how I all of a sudden disappeared from this city eight years ago today."

The police call Ben and he comes right over with his wife. At first they don't recognize me and Ben says "This guy isn't Charles Kenna. Did he have any papers on him?" and the policeman says "Not one."

"Ben," I say, "remember the fountain pen complete with ink in it no less that I gave you for your thirteenth birthday? And Jill, you can't forget the swanky dinner I treated you both to on your fifth wedding anniversary and the pram blanket I gave for Tippy the day she was born."

After they finish hugging me I say "Now tell the police if I was ever a liar or drunk in my life."

"One glass of wine at dinner," Ben says, "and one only. He always said he had to have a clear head and settled stomach for the next morning if he was to do his best at work, which he also took home weekends."

"And his word?" Jill says. "He never uttered anything but the absolute truth, just like his actions: a moralist not to be

believed. He used to make me ashamed of myself just for breathing, till I realized what a burden of unexamined guilt he must
be carrying on his head, and then I began feeling a bit sorry for
him.''

The police go see Ivy and Roz. They deny everything, I'm
told. "Charles Kenna? We've never known a Kenna or Kennan
or any kind of name like that in our lives. And the only male
to enter our apartment in thirty years was the super and he only
to fix things.''

The police tell me there's no proof I was ever in their apartment. "The sisters are known as eccentrics in the neighborhood,
mostly because they keep so much to themselves, but they've
never been in trouble with us or the city or anyone. Far as
visitors go, they said nobody but that super and a lonely spinster
friend from childhood who came twice a year for tea till she
died recently and a few times the upstairs neighbor who they
said came to the door for this or that, but no one else.''

"I don't remember the friend at all. As for the neighbor and
super, when she was at the door, I was bound and gagged
behind it, and when he came inside, I was locked in the bedroom.''

The police won't investigate further till I come up with more
evidence for them. My lawyer tells me if I take the sisters to
court I'll not only lose the case but be countersued for slander
and in both cases I'll have to pay their legal fees.

So I don't pursue it. I never had much savings, so have to
borrow from Ben and Jill to move into a hotel, get my teeth
fixed and keep myself going till I get back my health and buy
some clothes and find a job in my old field. All my belongings
were put on the street eight years ago after I didn't pay my rent
for three months.

A month after I'm released and when I'm still recuperating,
I get a phone call in my hotel room.

"Surprise, it's me," Roz says. "We only today got a telephone put in after all these years and I wanted you to be my first personal call."

"Oh boy, thanks loads, but how'd you find me?"

"There are only so many Charles Kennas in hotels, you know. How are you?"

"I'll tell you how I am, you witch. I'm getting stronger every day, so don't try to mess with me again, you understand? If I didn't think you had a lethal weapon of some kind or I'd get in serious trouble for it or at least could do it in a way where the police would never know, I'd club you both over the head till you woke up in hell."

"For what, dear?"

"For what? Hey, I know you're both out of your skulls, but this much?"

"Who you speaking to, love?" Ivy says, picking up what I suppose is the extension.

"Oh, some nice wrong number I got by mistake when I dialed the hardware store."

"If he's that nice ask him to come over for lunch and a chat. That's the main reason we got this contraption for, isn't it: to widen our social life?"

"I already did. He said no."

"I didn't hear you ask him."

"You were in the other room."

"But I was listening at the door."

"All right, maybe I didn't. My mind might be slipping, just like yours. Excuse me, sir, but could you? My sister and I are two extremely lonely though I think reasonably intelligent and interesting elderly ladies and would love to have male company for a change. We're quite honestly bored with each other and ourselves, which you must have picked up during our harmless hostile exchange just now."

"Maybe another day," I say. "But Ivy, you know damn well who this is, so how about an explanation from you or Roz as to why you put me through so much for eight years?"

"Explanation?" She laughs. "Oh you poor love. We thought it was obvious to you. And this is who I suggested we invite for lunch?"

"It wasn't obvious," I say. "Maybe my mind suffered some irreversible comprehensive damage or psychological breakdown or whatever it was while I was with you two, so explain to me slowly and clearly so I can once and for all understand rather than just rack my brains and guess."

"Explain what?" Roz says. "Why I dialed the wrong number? People make mistakes, that's all," and they hang up.

After that they phone me once a week at the hotel, always asking if this is that nice man they got by mistake a week ago . . . a couple of weeks ago . . . a month ago and so forth, and each time I say no and hang up. Then my health is back to normal. I find a job, rent an apartment, get an unlisted phone and stay away from their neighborhood and never hear from them again.

Said

He said, she said.

She left the room, he followed her.

He said, she said.

She locked herself in the bathroom, he slammed the door with his fists.

He said.

She said nothing.

He said.

He slammed the door with his fists, kicked the door bottom.

She said, he said, she said.

He batted the door with his shoulder, went into the kitchen, got a screwdriver, returned and started unscrewing the bathroom doorknob.

She said.

He said nothing, unscrewed the doorknob, pulled the doorknob out of the door, but the door stayed locked. He threw the doorknob against the door, picked it up and threw it down the hall, banged the door with the screwdriver handle, wedged the screwdriver blade between the door and jamb and tried forcing the door open. The blade broke, the door stayed locked.

He said, she said, he said.

He got about fifteen feet down the hall and charged at the door.

She said.

He stopped.

He said.

She said nothing. Then she said, he said, she said, he said.

He got about ten feet down the hall this time and charged at the door.

She said.

He crashed into the door with his shoulder, bounced off it and fell down. The top hinge came out of the jamb, the door opened on top, hung on its bottom hinge for a few seconds while he was on the floor screaming from his shoulder pain, then came out of the bottom hinge and fell on his head and bad shoulder as he was getting up.

She said.

He pushed the door over, fell down on his bad shoulder. The pain was so great now not only from the first crash and then the door falling on his shoulder but the shoulder hitting the floor, that his body did a kind of automatic reflex movement where his legs shot out and his head and shoulders hit the baseboard. He screamed even louder.

She said.

He kept on screaming.

She said.

He held his breath, started crying. His head was bleeding but didn't hurt. He looked at her sitting on the bathtub rim, got up, kicked the wall, kicked the door, screamed from the shoulder pain he already had and now more so from the kicking.

She said, he said.

She came out of the bathroom, looked at his head, looked at his shoulder, looked for a towel in the bathroom. The towels were on the rack now under the door on the floor. She grabbed the handkerchief sticking out of his pants pocket, put it in his good hand, put his hand with the handkerchief to his head wound, sat him on the toilet seat and went into the bedroom and phoned their doctor.

The receptionist said, she said, the receptionist said.

The doctor said, she said, the doctor said, she said.

She came back. The handkerchief was soaked with blood and he was whining and groaning. She ran down the hall, got a bath towel out of the linen closet, wrapped it around his head, put his coat over his good shoulder, got her wallet and keys, got his wallet and made sure his hospital insurance card was in it, held his good arm, walked him out of the apartment, down the three flights and out of the building and hailed a cab.

She said, the cabby said.

They got into the cab and started for the hospital. A few blocks from the hospital a car ran a red light and smashed into her side of the cab. The cab turned over and ended up on its wheels on the sidewalk. She forced his door open and the two of them stepped out of the cab, shaken but not hurt. The pain in his shoulder was gone. The towel had fallen off his head in the crash and the wound was no longer bleeding. The cabby's head had gone through the windshield and was bleeding a lot.

They forced open the cabby's door.

A pedestrian said, she said, the pedestrian said and ran to a public phone booth and dialed.

They carefully broke the glass around the cabby's head, pulled him back into the cab, rested his head on the man's coat. She took off her sweater and wrapped it around the cabby's head. A crowd had gathered around them.

The crowd said, she said, the crowd said.

The pedestrian came back and said.

The police came in a few minutes and right behind them, an ambulance.

The police said, she said, he said, the crowd said, the police said, the doctor and the ambulance attendant said, the police said.

The doctor examined the cabby, signaled the attendant to put him into the ambulance.

She said, the doctor said, she said.

The doctor looked at her husband's head wound and shoulder while the attendant and a policeman put the cabby on a stretcher and then into the back of the ambulance.

The doctor said, he said, she said.

The doctor got into the ambulance and the ambulance drove away.

The police said, they said, the police said, he said, she said.

A tow truck from the cab company pulled up. The tower hitched the cab to the truck, held up the bloody sweater and coat and said.

She said, took the sweater and coat and put the sweater into a trash can.

The tow truck drove off, the police drove away and the crowd broke up.

She said, he said.

He swung his arm and his shoulder still didn't hurt. She touched his shoulder gently and it still didn't hurt. He said, she shook her head. He touched his shoulder a little harder than she did and it still didn't hurt. He shook his head and smiled.

She said.

He nodded, looked sad and said.

She said, he said.

She took both his hands and kissed his cheek. He kissed her lips.

A passerby said.

He said.

The passerby laughed, waved his hand at them and walked on.

She hailed a cab.

She said, the cabby said, he said.

The cabby shrugged his shoulders and drove off. They started to walk home. A scavenger picked her sweater out of the trash can, held it up, said, dropped it back in and wiped her hands on a rag. She picked the sweater up with a stick this time and dropped it into one of her two bags.

A Sloppy Story

"Listen to this," I say. "This guy comes in and says to me and I say to him and he says and I say and the next thing I know he does this to me and I do that to him and he this and I that and a woman comes in and sees us and says and I say to her and he says to me and she to him and he says and does this to her and I say and do that to him and she doesn't say anything but does this and that to us both and then a second time and he says and she says and I say and we all do and say and that's it, the end, what happened, now what do you think?"

"It won't work," a man says. His partner says "It will work, I know it will," and I say "Please, gentlemen, make up your minds. Do you think it will work or not?" The first man says no and his partner yes and I clasp my hands in front of my chest hoping they'll agree it will work and give me money for it so I won't have to be broke anymore or at least not for the next year, when the phone rings and the first man picks up the receiver and says "Yuh?" The person on the other end says something and the man says "You're kidding me now, aren't you?" His partner says "Who is it, something important?" and the man says and his partner says "Just tell him to go fly away with his project, now and forever," and I just sit there and the man hangs up the phone and says to us "Now where were we?"

"I was," I say. "He was," his partner says. "Okay," he says, "Let's continue where we left off from, though quickly, as I got a long day," and we talk and he says "I still don't go for it," and his partner says "I'm starting to agree with you, now and forever," and I say "Please, gentlemen, let me tell the story over. Maybe it will be more convincing the second time around and I promise to be quicker about it," and I start the story from the beginning: guy coming in, says to me, me to him, does this, I do, woman, what we all said and did and then the partner, not agreeing, phone ringing, call ending, my retelling the story. After I finish I say "So what do you think? Will it work?"

"No," they both say and I say "Well, no harm in my having tried, I guess," and the first man says "No harm is right except for our precious lost time," and sticks out his hand and I shake it and shake his partner's hand and say "Can I use your men's room before I go? It might be my last chance for a while." His partner says "Second door to the right on your way out to the elevator," and I say "Which way is the elevator again, left or right when I get out of your office?" and he says and I say "Thanks," and they say and I leave, wave goodbye to the receptionist, go to the men's room on their floor, take the elevator down, go through the building's lobby to the street. It's a nice day, finally. It was raining heavily when I came in. My umbrella! Damn, left it upstairs, should I go back for it? No. Yes. What the hell, why not, it's not an old umbrella, it's still a good serviceable umbrella. And if I don't get it I'll have to buy a new umbrella at probably twice what the one upstairs cost me three years ago the way inflation's going crazy today.

I go back through the lobby, elevator, get on it, upstairs, their floor, past the men's room, into their office and the receptionist says and I say, "I know, but I," and point to it and the partners come out of the room we were talking in before just as I grab my umbrella and look at me but don't say anything when I say hello but just walk into another room and I say goodbye to the receptionist and she nods at me and starts typing rapidly and I leave the office, elevator, lobby and see it's raining heavily again. Rain coming down like, streets filled with water like, people running out of the rain like, sky like, traffic like, I open the umbrella and walk in the rain totally protected because of my umbrella, long raincoat and boots and think "Well, I at least did one thing right today and that's going back for the umbrella, and maybe one other thing and that's wearing the right rain clothes," when someone ducks under my umbrella, a woman, hair soaked by the rain, and says "Mind if I walk with you as far as the bank on the corner? It closes in a few minutes and I have to put in some money by today."

"Sure," I say and we walk, I hold the umbrella, she her coat together at the collar, and talk, she "Can we walk faster?" I say sure, she asks where I was going, I say to an office building a block past her bank, she asks, I tell her, she says "Well what do you know," because it seems she's a good friend of the very man I want to see most about the same story project I spoke to those partners about, but whom I haven't been able to get an appointment with for more than a month. So I suggest, she says "Yes, but let me get done with my bank first," goes in, comes out, we have coffee at a coffee shop across the street, she asks, I tell, starting with the guy who comes in and says and I say and we do and the woman and all we said and did and then the partners, men's room, lobby, sunshine, umbrella, should I? shouldn't I? upstairs, receptionist and partners again, I retrieve, I leave, typing rapidly, raining heavily, everything looking like something else, open the umbrella, woman ducks under, though at first I didn't think it was a woman, I thought it was a mugger, walk, talk, faster, she asks, I say, well what do you know, she knows so and so, I suggest, she says yes, bank, coffee shop and coffees. "So what do you think?" I say. "Your friend will like it or am I fooling myself?"

"If he doesn't like it he ought to change professions," she says and borrows a coin from me, makes a phone call, comes back, "He says to hustle right over," we do, elevator, office, receptionist, secretary, big how do you do from her friend who I tell the whole story to from the beginning, he says "Better than I expected even from what Pam told me it would be over the phone. I'll take it," and we shake hands, sign a contract, he writes out a check, we drink champagne to our future success, Pam and I leave, downstairs, lobby, sunny outside. Oh my God, I think, I forgot my umbrella again. "Oh my God," I say, "I left my umbrella upstairs."

"Leave it," she says, "since you now have enough money to buy ten umbrellas. Twenty if you want, though I don't know why you would." "True," I say. "Want to go for another coffee?" "Coffee?" she says. "I think a drink's more what we deserve. I know I sure do after what I just did for you." "True," I say, "and we'll go to the best place possible," and we start walking. Sun goes, clouds come, we walk faster, looking for a classier bar than the three we pass, but not fast enough, as the rain suddenly comes, drenching us before we can find protection from it.

"I knew I should have gone up for my umbrella," I say. "So we're wet," she says. "So what? It'll make the day more memorable for you. In fact, what I'd do if I were you, just to make the day one of the most memorable of your life, is—" but I cut her off and say "I know, I might," and she says "Not you might, you should," and I say "I know, I will," and she smiles, I smile, we take each other's hands, put our arms around each other's waists, "Let's," she says, "Let's," I say, and run out from under the awning into the rain. "Dad, look at those crazy people getting wet," a boy says, protected by his father's umbrella.

"You know what I want most of all now that I've sold my story project?" I say to her, standing in the pouring rain and holding and hugging her and looking over her shoulder at the boy being pulled along by his father because he wants to stay and watch us and she says "What?" and I tell her and she says and I say "And also to eventually walk in the pouring rain with an umbrella over my future wife and me and future daughter or son, but with the child being around that boy's age." "Why an umbrella?" she says and I say and she says "Silly, you don't get colds that way," and I say and she says "No," and I say "Oh." Just then a cab drives by too close to the curb and splashes us up to our waists and I start cursing and shaking my fist at it and she says and I say "You're right, raincoats and all we're already slopping wet," and we laugh and go into a bar a half-block away and order a glass of wine each.

"What are you two so happy about," the bartender says, "besides getting yourselves dripping wet and probably catching your death?" and I say "Really interested?" and he says "Interested," and I say "Then I'll tell you," and do, starting from the time the man came in, woman, partners, office, men's room, lobby, sunny again, umbrella and rain, woman and bank, coffees, what do you know, so and so, deal, champagne, check, no umbrella, mixing the story up a little here and there, sun goes, rain falls, running through it, father and son, my thoughts and wants, bar, drinks, bartender and he says "That story rates a drink on the house if I ever heard one," and pours some more wine into our glasses, we toast and drink, he holds up his glass of soda water, people coming in ask what the celebration's about, I tell them, from beginning to end, leaving a little out now and then. "Very interesting," one of them says and buys us another wine each. By that time the rain's stopped but we're not dry yet and I say to Pam "Let's make it a perfect end to a great day," and she says "No, really, I've had a change of mind, besides my boyfriend waiting at home," and goes.

Just then a man comes in and I say "You wouldn't believe—" and he says "Wouldn't believe what? Because if you think you've something to say, listen to my story first," and he tells me about his wife who suddenly left him last week same day his dad got a coronary and his dog ran away and I say "Excuse me, you're right, and I think I better get home before it rains again," and I get off the stool. "Wait," he says, "you haven't heard the worst of it yet," but I'm out the door, rain's started again, I hail a cab, feel in my pockets, no wallet, wave the cab away and walk the two miles to my home. Phone's ringing when I enter the apartment. It's the man who bought my story project. He says "Tear up that check and contract as I just received a cable from overseas that says our company's gone bankrupt." I shout "Liar." He says "Not so." I slam down the receiver, am shivering, sneezing, want to get into a hot tub, but for some reason the water only runs cold.

Magna . . . Reading

Stop, go, don't write anymore. She's downstairs reading my work. Stop, go, don't don't write anything anymore. Reading what I've written the last two months. Stop, go, go for more, get another quick one in while she's reading my work, anything to relieve the, divert the, take my mind off the anxious feelings I have about her reading my work. Because she is reading my work. I hear a page turning. I heard a groan before. I heard a few laughs before. I heard pages turning before. First one's twelve pages, next is six pages, one after that's eight pages, last one I completed today, actually completed it yesterday but rewrote the last page today so I suppose I can say I completed it today, anyway that one's sixteen pages. She's reading them all: all the stories, all the pages. Stop, go, just write some more. Fill up this page, go right on to another. How many pages more will it take to make a story, have one ready for her when she finishes the other four, run downstairs, while she's coming into the house and about to walk or run upstairs, and wave the new one at her, this one, and say stop, don't come up, stay down there, go back to the porch, here's another one I want you to read, the first draft of something I just this moment completed, in fact maybe I won't rewrite it at all, so this is perhaps the completed story, because I've always in the past rewritten the first draft of my stories, all two-fifty to three hundred of them, and this one I want to be just a little bit different than the rest, a story in its more natural and raw form, the first draft, so here it is, don't come up, I said stop, not another step, go back, where are your glasses? you leave them on the porch? well put them on, rather, go outside, sit down in the chaise longue again, put on your glasses and read this, it's short so shouldn't take long.

No thanks, she said.

Thank you but no, she said.

No, I don't really think I could read it right now, she said, But thanks.

No, really, please, though you have my thanks for offering me another story, I doubt I could read one more, she says.

No, I'm sorry, Willy, really, but I can't, and not because I don't want to or because I couldn't bear to read another of your stories, but because my eyes are too tired to, Magna says, And that's the honest truth.

No, really, it's impossible, out of the question, and not because I'm too tired to or my eyes are too damaged to or any of those why-I-can't-read-another-of-Willy's-stories stories, Magna says, But because I just don't, won't and will probably not— not probably not—I will never again want to read one of them, plain as that, which I'm not a bit sorry to say so, and you want to know why?

Why you're not a bit sorry to say so? I say.

Why I don't want to read another of your stories, she says,— You want to know why?

No, I say.

No I don't, I say.

No really, thanks, but spare me, I say.

I don't know—I think I do but then again I think I don't, I say.

Yes, I think I do, I say, Why?

All right, I say, Why?

Why? I say.

Yes, I say, I really would like to know why. Why?

You bet I want to know why, I say.

Why can't you read another one of my stories? I say. Just tell me, give me one good reason, give me even half a good reason, because what else do you have to do or do you do? Other than reading my stories you do nothing but sit in a chair and sleep in bed or sit up in bed and sleep in a chair, so you're in fact lucky I give you my stories to read, you're in fact lucky I keep writing stories which you're then lucky I give you them to read, because if I stopped writing them you of course wouldn't have any more to read, and then what else would you have to do but sit and sleep, in bed or in a chair?

I wish I could read one more, Willy, she said, But I busted my glasses today and don't have another pair.

All you do is give excuses, I said, Other than for sitting in bed and sleeping in a chair and vice versa, and of course reading my stories, in bed or in a chair.

I'd love to read your story, she said, But not outside. It's dark now, can't you see? Actually, I don't want to read your story and it isn't dark, and don't ask me why I made up such a ridiculous excuse when you can see from here it's still very much light out, or said I'd ever want to read your story, if I did, though that's all I'm going to say of it, now and for all time about your story and giving excuses for not reading them, even if that last excuse is way less than insufficient for you.

I wish I could read another of your stories, Magna said. In fact I wish I could read a couple-hundred more. But you won't believe this—I can't see. I suddenly lost all my sight.

I'd love more than anything in the world to read another of your stories, Willy, Magna says, But you won't believe this in a hundred thousand years: I can't see now and never could.

She's still reading my stories, pages are still being turned, grunts, groans, laughs, still being made, it's still light out, sunny and bright, and she's still sitting in the chaise longue on the back porch of this cottage overlooking the ocean—the top floor of the cottage does, all she can see from the porch in that direction are the trees obscuring the ocean—one of the cats in her lap, other two cats under the chaise longue—reading, reading my stories—she is, the cats if they're still where they were when I last saw them are probably still sleeping—while I try to write another story so she'll have a fifth one of mine to read in the order I wrote them, one in May, two in June, one in July, all in the same year, and this one if I finish it on time written the same day I finished the last page of the fourth story, and now of a length where I can at last say—well, maybe I could have said it two to three pages back—that if I have to stop because she's opening the screen door to come upstairs to tell me what she thinks of my four stories, it'll at least be, if not finished, then long enough to be considered in some circles a story, and maybe finished even if I stop in the middle of a sentence or anywhere but the end of the sentence in a place where to many readers in some circles if not most readers in many circles to every single reader in every circle, a story that's unfinished, or rather, a story that perhaps to some or all readers is unfinished but to me is—

I stopped writing that last sentence because it was getting confusing. Not Getting: it was confusing. Is confusing, so long as I still have it on this page. But what I meant to say in the sentence or two before the one before the last one was that no matter where I stop, the story will be finished, since that's the kind of story I've decided this one will be: a story that will be finished, if I don't finish it before then with a period at the end of a final paragraph, the second she opens the screen door to come upstairs with the other four stories to talk about them. How do I know she'll come upstairs with the other stories and will want to talk about them? That she'll even open the screen door? That she'll even finish the stories? That she'll even finish one of the pages of one of the stories or even the first paragraph or line or word of one of the stories? That she'll even—uh oh, I just heard the screen door open. I know I said I'd stop the second she opened the door to come upstairs, but I'm not sure she was the one who opened the door. It could be one of her cats. Each one knows how to open the screen door if it's not locked. They open the screen door, and have opened it this way hundreds of times before, by pushing one paw between the door and jamb till they get

The Last

I want to throw the whole thing into the river. I think I've already said that. Or I've done that. Which is it? Me mind, me mind. Been working at this so long I forget what I do, why I do it, when I did it. Let me see, when was it? I was, well there I was, I mean it was, oh forget it. I'll never remember, but give it one more shot. I had this thing, right, this thing and threw it into the river, there it was, floating for a while, sank after a while, so be it. But what was that thing? I thought I said. Let me think. No you didn't. It was a thing, right. It was it. It was this. I mean—looking over to where this thing is or was—it isn't there so it was my manuscript. That's what it was. There. To be exact: my biggest manuscript. That's exactly what it was. Threw the damn thing into the river. Wrote about it, wrote it, wrote what I did with it after I wrote it: river, manuscript. Wrote that I was finished with it, had enough, couldn't go on with it, that's what I felt, that's what I did, threw it into the river, the whole thing, so what more's to be said about it, right? I guess nothing, so I'll sign off.

But now I've nothing to do. It's like a child who's upped and gone away from home, just left, left home for good, deserted the hearth, said to its daddy, me, I'm leaving for good, said to its mommy, me, I've had it here forever, said to its parents, me,

because I did it, I'm responsible, I gave birth to it, I suckled it,
I provided the egg and sperm and place to grow, I nurtured it,
I brought it up, I got its food and fed its face, I took care of it
when it was sick, I cut its cord with my teeth, bit through it
and sewed it up, I read it its first words, taught it how to talk
and walk, held it against my chest, held it to my breast, I wiped
its ass every day and night eight-ten times a day and threw out
its shit, I let it piss on my head and toes, I let it pull my nose
and lobes, I held and kissed it, I was held and kissed by it, I
am lost without it, I walk around town wondering where it is
and what I'll do for the rest of my life without it, I, well, I
can't, well I just can't live without it I sometimes think.

So I start something else. I find another woman. Or continue
with the previous figure of speech. A woman finds another man.
She gets him to pump into her when she's ready to conceive. It
doesn't work the first or second or even the third time so she
gets him to keep pumping into her every day and night till he's
sure she can't do anything but conceive. He and she conceive.
They do. I do with my woman and man. We conceive. I'm
they. She has, I have, we do, a baby. Another one—our second—end of figure of speech. A fine figure of speech. An awful
figure of speech. I'm not even sure it was a figure of speech.
But we have, it is, I start, again and again. Work on it day and
night, night and day, days and nights, and what then? What
could I expect? It runs off. Leaves the house. It leaves us. Be
more direct. Another unfinished—yes? Goddamn novel, that's
what it was. There it is. Why wasn't I that specific at first? Now
I have been, so what's the dif? Ran off, left me, left us, gone,
where to? The river. There it goes. Someone save it. Please,
anyone, it's drowning, I can't swim, a man jumps in, woman
too, he sinks but she swims a couple of strokes, says I can't
make it so far to get him and it both, swims back dragging the
man with her to land. So I jump in with my shoes on, jump
and swim but it's gone, what can I say? Murky as this river is,

this body of water is, this figure of speech is, I still dive and dive and dive till I decide the water's too murky and I'll never find it no matter how many times I dive, so I swim to shore, where I am now, drying off, manuscript gone.

So what do I do but start another one. Use my penis and vagina, testes and ova. Doesn't work. Nothing produced. We're infertile, she's barren, I've little to no sperm count, she's lost count, I'm barren, she's infertile, whatever it is, or we are, nothing comes, though it's fun, so damn much fun, but not another fetus, no more children, not even a part of one manuscript, I'm done, can't last like this for that long without another one, so might as well chuck it all in, jump into the river myself, which I do, we.

Together we jump. Holding hands. What else is there to do now? Can't do anything but what we can do I suppose, though I don't know—I'm not very good with those—but anyway, it's what we do, jump into the river, we know it's over our heads, heard of others who've jumped into it from the same spot we did and sank ten feet or so over their heads, so we've jumped, hand in hand, not a very long jump, fifteen feet at the most, not even as long as that, twelve, ten, we jump, fall, end up in the river, sink, about eight feet so two to three feet over our heads, we're done, wasn't fun, drowning wasn't, falling was quite a thrill, but drowning was dreadful, couldn't breathe, choked to death, gagged when I lost my last breathe, I'm not sure if it was my last, drowning was agonizing, though, never again.

So I watch all this from my window. Watch the river through the only window of my apartment, a good apartment despite just a single room and its shortage of space and what might be called a dining alcove: right on the river, window with a broad view. Once though, it's true, I threw my manuscript into the river, no one jumped after it. I sure didn't. Just threw it out the window into the river. It can be done if the manuscript's heavy enough and I give it a good toss. But that was it. Sank, didn't float. None of the pages came up. Maybe somewhere one did, but never here, far as I know, and none was ever found anywhere else, far as I know too. Now I look out this window. Water. Bridges. River traffic. Ships, barges, tugs. A pleasure craft. Flock of geese or ducks go past flying south though at this time of the year I'd think it'd be north. Workers on the docks way off. Nearer me, and below, people on the promenade. Mothers, carriages, nannies, men reading on benches, and so on. Boys and girls skipping by and jumping rope. In the sky: planes, clouds. A beautiful day. White clouds, blue sky, setting sun. Quite a sight. And before me, nothing. Meaning in my typewriter or at the end of my pen, nothing. Time maybe for me to go. No. Out the window first. I look. I open it. Mild as it looks. The pen. From three stories up I throw it into the river. It makes a blip and is gone. Now the typewriter. Too heavy to throw. I go downstairs, cross the promenade, dump it over the railing. Drop it over, really. Plop. Gone. I thought it'd make a louder sound. A woman jogs by. "What'd you drop in the river," she says on the run, "your newborn child?" Wow, that's a strange thing to say. Even if she saw what I dropped and knew what I'd been thinking, which I'm sure she didn't, a very strange remark. That woman must be crazy.

Ten Years—

Earlier today he threw out his father's old bathrobe and wants
to tell—

She isn't home by six and at seven he starts to get—

He dials her office and—

At eight the phone rings—

She unlocks the door around—

He kisses her, wants to know what—

She says "It was unfortunate but late this afternoon a lawyer
from Abadine and Lynch"—

"I don't care what the hell happened, the least you"—

"I'm sorry too, and I'm telling you, I would have called much
sooner but"—

All right, that's over, and he realizes he got overexcited when
the right reaction—

"Are you still hungry?" he—

"To tell you the truth, Smitty, I only want"—

"Do what you want, what do I care, because nobody here"—

"Now listen, I don't want to"—

"But two hours," he says, "two"—

"I thought we went"—

"We did, but still—oh, what am I getting so damn upset"—

"That's what I feel, though I've absolutely said my last on it tonight," and she goes—

"Wait, we haven't"—

He hears the shower—

He goes into the kitchen and gets himself—

In the kitchen he wonders if—

He opens the back door to his floor's service area to see if the garbage—

Good, and he picks up the plastic bag and brings it back into—

He opens it and first has to take some garbage out before—

He shakes it out, wipes off a little meat sauce from—

He pours himself another drink and looks at the bathrobe lying—

It's still wearable, so why did—

Because the collar's so frayed and the cuffs also and the belt almost a string now and besides that—

When did his mother buy—

He remembers when his father was very sick and wore this robe and the spittle would—

He'd have to wipe it off the sleeves and the collar and the front—

"Dad," he'd say then, "when you feel the drool"—

"I can't help it," his father would say, "I can't help it, and it's not"—

"You can make an attempt to help if you'd only"—

"Stop pestering me, stop ordering"—

How many years did he live with them then, helping his mother take care of him, and people, especially his sisters, saying he was too old to live home again but that they—

For the last year of his life his father was either in this bathrobe or—

First thing every morning he'd lift his father off the bed, stand him up, put the bathrobe on him, walk him to—

His wife comes into the kitchen, is in her nightgown, and says as she—

"Excuse me, but why's the garbage"—

"I'll clean it up, don't worry"—

"And why's the old robe"—

"I threw it out today and wanted to keep it thrown out but"—

"Why'd you"—

"I just didn't"—

"It's actually too worn to wear and probably has"—

"You can't know how many, and it was really the reason I jumped all over"—

"Look, Smitty, that's all"—

"I wanted to explain, though, and I suppose I was lucky the guy who picks up the trash at six"—

"I'm not sure how lucky you"—

"Maybe I can bring it to"—

"It's beyond"—

"Ah, best thing is to get rid of it, right? but before I do, maybe I could"—

"Where are you going"—

"In my wallet, or, though this must sound infantile—maudlin's more like it—in"—

"Not 'maudlin' or 'infantile' as much as"—

"I want to remember the design and colors and"—

"Maybe it's a good idea then, but anyway, mind if"—

"Sure, I'll just stay here a few more minutes and make my decision, and clean up, of"—

"I wish you'd do that now, for it's beginning"—

"Goodnight, lovey"—

He pours—

The cat jumps off the refrigerator and immediately—

"Get off it, Lucy, get"—

Oh what the hell, he—

"Hey, Lucy, hey, baby—hey, stupid Lucy, you didn't eat"—
He picks up—
"I'm sorry, I didn't mean"—
Maybe he should just go to bed—
No, the bathrobe, and the garbage—he has to deal with them, and he rips a few paper towels off the—
He fastens the top of the garbage bag with the tab, puts the bag back in the service area, locks the door, thinks Why not the newspapers too? puts a pile of newspapers and magazines under the garbage bag, pokes the bag and it doesn't slide off, locks the door, downs his—
It was for winter anyway and—
That's not the reason, of course, since he could easily—
A few weeks after his father died, his mother—
He said "I don't want to hear of it, I"—
It hung in her—
A few months after that his mother said "I've had it cleaned and if you don't"—
He took it home—
He picks the cat up off the bathrobe and sits her on—
The bathrobe hung in their—
His wife said a number of times—
He covered it with a plastic bag from a dry cleaner just so—
Then one night when it was almost zero degree out and the wind off the river—
The robe kept him warm but always reminded—
Out, he has to throw it out, he has to get rid of the damn thing once and for—
His wife comes in and says "At least you cleaned"—
"I'm having trouble deciding"—
"Want me"—
"No, I'll"—
"Do or don't—really, what's the big deal of one or two more days, and this time I'm going to"—

"I'll be there"—

She—

He picks up—

The cat follows—

"Say, lady, don't you have"—

Oh, maybe one more time, and he takes off his—

He shakes out the robe, the cat runs under—

It still feels—

He starts crying, wipes his eyes—

He puts it—

What is it about some things, the memory of—

Maybe he should just rip it to pieces, at least rip the sleeves off his—

It was hanging on the outside of the closet door of his father's room the morning his mother yelled to—

He ran in, took his father's hand, bent over him while—

She was already—

He said "Wait, wait, maybe"—

He put his ear—

She said "I'm afraid I did"—

"And his"—

"Took it"—

"Maybe you should phone"—

She didn't—

"I'll do it, but maybe you should leave"—

When he came back into the room he held her and said "You have to know you did everything"—

"We did"—

"And that it was really much better we took care of him at"—

"Believe me, dear"—

Two or three days later, while they were sitting in mourning at home, he—

His aunt said "I was wondering what it"—

His mother said "Honestly, I didn't even"—

He put—

That was almost ten years—

He takes off the bathrobe, gets a hanger from the front closet and slips it into the shoulders of the robe, takes a winter coat off another hanger and puts it over—

As he's walking away from the closet he hears—

He picks up the coat and robe off the floor, gets a wooden—

Maybe he should just forget it, because he knows what he's going to do with it eventually, and he takes the robe out from under the coat—

No, he can't just now and that's all there is—

"Smitty"—

"Be there"—

He hangs the robe on a wire—

He brushes his teeth, goes to the bedroom and gets in—

He says "I'm so mad at myself for being unable"—

"Don't worry about"—

"But it"—

"Please, sweetheart"—

"I just wish the guy would"—

"You're referring to"—

"I'm not 'referring'—I'm talking about him, yes, because"—

"Really, it's so natural to act like that, so why knock"—

"But what's this crazy hold"—

"Shh, sleep, I'd like to talk more but I swear"—

"Anyway, tomorrow I'm"—

"Good, she'll"—

"And if she wants to, maybe we'll go over for a drink and take her"—

"Fine, fine, but"—

"No, goddamnit—I mean, we will take her out, but now"—

"Where are"—

He leaves it on top of the newspaper pile outside the service door and says "Look, this in no way reflects—I mean, I'm not saying goodbye for all time by doing this and in this particular way, but—well, of course I'm not, because all I'm saying is that this damn thing of yours—oh hell," and he goes inside and gets a pair—

"No!" and he locks the door, puts the scissors away and goes into—

The Cove

Two men are walking toward each other on a beach. One man's holding a girl of nine months and the other man's with a woman and four children between the ages of seven to twelve. The two men are eyeing each other. The man with the baby wonders who these people are and where they're staying on the point. He comes down to this beach every day and maybe two and three times a day and if he sees one person in a week on it it's a lot. No, wrongly worded, or something's wrong. Go back. Two men, beach, which is really a cove, cove which the man with the baby rents the same cottage on every summer, or to be more exact: the cove is part of the cottage's property and the cottage is about 200 feet into the woods. Something like that. Doesn't right now have to be that exact. The other man's staying with his mother and stepfather for two weeks and the woman is his wife and the children are their grandchildren and the stepfather, who's been married to this man's mother for more than forty years, has a house on the next cove, or rather, owns the entire next cove, which is about a half mile long, and the house, or compound, for it consists of three houses besides the enormous main house, all situated fairly close together, and two garages and several barns and sheds and a private studio, is about a mile from the stepfather's cove. To get to their cove they drove a car down their road to it, or that's what the man with the baby assumes, if these people are who he now thinks they are: the ones who walked along this cove two summers ago, stopped to look at the lopsided vandalized boathouse and when he later asked his wife who they could be, she told him. To get to his cove the man with the baby walked to it. Mosquitoes, what's left of the black flies, the sound of a large animal in the woods. Probably a porcupine—he and his wife have seen one around the cottage the last two days. Hotter and more humid than is usual around here during any part of the summer and it's just the end of June and not even ten a.m. Maine, some hundred-fifty miles from the Canadian border along the coast. The man with the woman and children and the man with the baby are now only about fifty feet apart. One of the children has a dog on a leash and the dog starts growling at the man with the baby. The man with the baby thinks these must be the people he heard from his porch yesterday, talking loud and laughing and shrieking. The man with the woman and children thinks could this be Magna's new husband? He heard from his stepfather she got married a year and a half ago and had a baby over the winter. It must be, who else could it be? He met her alone on this beach several years ago, had a long talk with her, found they had many university acquaintances in common, thought her very smart, personable and attractive. His stepfather learned of her baby from the caretaker of her cottage. She's been renting that cottage for ten years or so, with this man for five years. He's been spending a week to two at one of his stepfather's guesthouses with his grandchildren and before that with his children and before that just with his wife, every other year and occasionally two years in a row for the last thirty-seven years. He brought his wife here thirty-eight years ago when they were engaged. They stayed in the main house—there were no guesthouses then— and on different floors. He remembers his stepfather calling him aside and saying "Your mother and I separated you two for very good reasons and we don't want either of you transversing the other's room any time of the day." Yesterday his wife said she was fed up looking after their grandchildren every summer for a week to two and especially every second year when they also have to deal with his aging mother and controlling stepfather. "I know I said this last summer, but this summer I mean it when I say it's the last time. I think I finally want those two weeks for ourselves, or if it has to be, then just for me." The man with the baby says "Hiya" to the first two children who pass and "Looks like your dog's a good watchdog by the way he growled."

"He's not our dog," the girl walking with the boy who's holding the leash says, "—he's our grandparents'," and she points to the two adults behind her.

"Oh, they're so young I thought they were your parents."

"No, our grandparents. Our parents are vacationing in France."

By this time the two older children have passed him and he says "Hi" and one of them says "Hi" and the other waves. He says hello to the woman as she passes. She smiles, says "Good morning," and continues walking. He says hello to the man who's about ten feet behind the woman, holding a long bleached branch he must have found on the beach and is using as a walking stick. The man says "Must seem like Times Square to you today."

"Why," the man with the baby says, stopping, "because it's so crowded or so hot?"

"Crowded for this particular beach and maybe because it's so hot. Didn't think of heat as such when I said it, nor have I been to New York in the summer to know how hot it gets, but it could be true too. How do you do?" He switches the stick to his left hand and puts out his free hand to shake. "Benton." They shake. "And who's this tyke?"

"Stella. I'm Will Taub. You people staying around here?"

"Turner Haskell's my stepfather. We're here with our grand-children for our biannual pilgrimage for a week. And you?"

"My wife and I are in the cottage that belongs to that decrepit boathouse there."

"Is this Magna's baby?" the woman says, coming back. The children continue to the end of the cove. "Hello, I'm Nicole. How is Magna? We heard she had a baby, and it's so darling—aren't you, you little dear." She puts her finger into the baby's hand which squeezes around it. "Ned, you remember Magna—she studied with Byron Parks."

"Sure, now I do—once had a very nice conversation with her on this beach."

"Boy, girl?" she asks Will.

"Stella," Ned says.

"Right. And Magna's just fine—up in the cottage now.—Better watch it—she collects fingers."

"She looks like Magna," she says. "Features, complexion, hair—everything."

"Whenever I hold her—of course the hair is another matter—people say she looks like Magna. And when she holds her"—no, all wrong, or mostly. Go back again. Two men, one holding a baby, other walking a dog. No, one's alone, other's with a dog. The woman and children are with his stepfather in the main house. The baby's with Magna. The men are walking toward each other on the cove that belongs to the cottage the man alone's renting. The dog barks at him from about thirty feet away, growls and bares its teeth when the men are ten feet apart. The man with the dog says "Whoa, Cunningham, whoa, boy, whoa," and has to pull the leash back with both hands. The dog's a retriever. The man alone says "Good morning. Looks like you have a pretty good watchdog there, but tell him I'm unarmed." "Oh, he's just a yipper—won't bite a flea. Cove must seem like Times Square to you today."

"With all this traffic?"

"I meant 'hot.' They're supposedly having, though a lot worse than ours, a heat spell in New York, the radio said, but maybe I got it all wrong. Because my assumption has always been that Times Square, because it's the most congested area in New York, would also be the hottest during a heat wave."

"Actually, it isn't the most congested. Fifty-seventh and Sixth, for instance, or Forty-second and Lex, as another example, are probably way more"—No, still all wrong, or mostly. "And that is where you're from, isn't it?" the man with the dog says, or without one. Just two men without baby, dog, stick or anything who have walked toward each other from opposite ends of the cove. "You're Magna's husband if I'm not mistaken, and according to my stepfather, Turner Haskell, you drove up from there a few days ago."

"Oh, how do you do, I'm Will Taub. We've been meaning to drop in to say hello to Mr. Haskell, but we've been so busy with a million things that we haven't had time yet. But where do you know Magna from—summers here?"

"Summers, once or twice—we only visit for a week every other year—though also through colleagues and mutual friends. My wife's in her field. We hear you had a baby over the winter."

"Nine months tomorrow—a girl. In fact, babyproofing entails half the million things we've been doing"—No, back again, just about everything's wrong. One man's on the beach, holding his baby girl. He's standing in the middle of the cove in front of his dilapidated boathouse. He and his wife and child drove up from New York two days ago and this is the first chance he's had to come down to the beach. Unpacking, shopping, cleaning, babyproofing the porch and house, putting up the mailbox, cutting back the alder, mowing, getting the lawnmower repaired, buying a washer and dryer, clearing a path to the woodshed and one to the beach. He's been coming to this cottage for the last five summers. His wife started renting it three summers before that. The cottage wasn't lived in for twenty years before she convinced the owners, who also had a winterized house in town, to let her open it. They thought nobody would want to live in it because everything in it was made or bought sixty years ago and the cottage was so run-down. She fixed it up, had part of the cottage rewired, bought a new water pump. Something like that. A phone installed, and also an electric stove. The rent was that cheap. He only knows of this part of Maine because of his wife. She started coming to it six years before he met her. Six and a half to be exact. They met in November, the following June they flew to Bangor, rented a car at the airport and drove to the cottage. Now they own a car. They'd like to buy the cottage. They've lived in Baltimore for the last two years but stayed for a week with his wife's parents in New York. His wife first came to this peninsula to visit her dissertation adviser and his family. That professor and his wife have since split up and sold their cottage. The man with the baby and his wife also teach and are on vacation for the next two months. The professor visited them here last year and his former wife will stay a week with them this summer. Go back. He and his child are on a beach, forget about getting there, why they're there—they are there. Man and baby, or just he's there. He took the baby down before but it was too hot and sunny for her—he forgot her bonnet—so he brought her back to the cottage, left her with his wife on the fenced-in porch, and went back to the beach. The beach there is a cove that's part of the property they rent. He sees at the end of the cove a man sitting on a rock and looking at the lighthouse in the bay. The end of the cove is called something but he forgets the word. The arm, promontory, reach—none of those. The "end of the cove" will do. It extends into the water, is shaped like the end of a crescent and is the beginning of the next cove in that direction. Will's in the middle of this cove, his cove. The man's sitting and looking out at the water. Maybe the man's looking at the lighthouse which is on an island about a mile away. The man stands and starts walking toward Will. If the man keeps walking at that regular pace it should take him several minutes to reach Will. Less, of course, if Will walks toward him and the man continues walking. Will walks toward the man, but only because he did come down to the beach to walk. To go from cove to cove and then after resting at the end of one, to go back. He could walk in the other direction and would prefer to, since he doesn't like meeting strangers on the beach, but the sun would be facing him. It'll be facing him coming back, but because of the reason he came down to walk on the beach, he wants to avoid the sun now more than he wants to avoid the stranger. So the man who was sitting at the end of the cove is now walking toward Will. He wonders who the man coming toward him is. Will wonders the same thing about the man. The man thinks Jesus, it's hot, why the hell did he ever come down here? He'll be glad when he gets back to the house. Will thinks he should've stayed on the shaded part of the porch. But he wanted to get away from the cottage, to take a long walk and let his mind wander. What comes into his head is that he left hot Baltimore to stay for a week in hot New York to come to an even hotter Maine. But it'll be mostly pleasant during the days and nights for the next two months while in Baltimore and New York it won't. The hot sticky weather must be traveling north because the radio this morning said that fairer drier weather was predicted for New York tomorrow and for New Hampshire the day after and for this part of Maine the day after that. The temperature and humidity when they left New York two days ago was in the mid-nineties. When they stopped for the night at a motel just over the Maine-New Hampshire border the weather was about the same as it was in New York. When they got to the cottage yesterday—No, he has his days mixed up. They got to the cottage two days ago, left New York the day before that. Today was the first chance he had to come down to the beach. The man's a few feet from him now and says hello. Will says hello.

"Hot enough for you?" the man says, neither of them stopping.

"I'll tell you, worse than it was where I drove up from."

They've smiled at one another, now pass one another. Will continues to the end of the cove. The man continues to the other end. Every now and then one of them looks back at the other. One time each looks back at about the same time and sees the other looking at him.

"Caught me," Will says.

Just looking, the other man thinks—not having much else to do, so just looking. But he doubts, knowing what he knows about him and his wife, that he's the type to mind somebody crossing his beach property which really isn't his. Which really isn't anybody's but everybody's, one could say. Say, that's not bad, even if he really means from the high water mark down. He just wishes his stepfather was the type to also believe it.

The man continues to the end of the cove and then goes around it and heads for the stairs in the middle of his stepfather's cove. When Will looks back again he doesn't see the man. On the next cove, he thinks. For a while he didn't want to look back because he didn't want to get caught again and have the man think he was spying on him. The man looks back again but only when he hears a seagull squawking. The gull flies over his head, dives to about fifteen feet of him, sweeps up, circles him twice—all the time squawking fiercely at him—and then flies back to the end of the cove and settles on a rock and seems to stare at him. He must have got too close to its nest, he thinks, when eggs or chicks were in it. Then he turns back to the stairs when he hears his grandchildren approaching them from the road. No, go back again. Two men. Maine. Its northern coast. Hot. Humid. Morning. Beach. Cove. Lobster boat dropping a trap about three hundred feet out in the water. No. One man, no boat, dusk, northern coast, cooler, orange-green striped sky. The man sits on a rock in front of a boathouse in the middle of the cove. He's tired. He did a lot of work today. Fenced in the porch, built two gates for it, scythed the overgrown grass around the cottage and then mowed it, two car trips to a town twenty miles away to get fencing and gate materials and a lawnmower part. He's holding a gin and tonic. He's showered and changed clothes and in a half-hour he'll have dinner. He's already cooked for his wife and himself and all he has to do when he gets back to the cottage is heat up the pot on the stove and take out the pan in the oven. He looks at the lobster boat in the water. Too far from shore and late in the day to be lobstering so probably going home. He thinks of the man he saw on the cove before. He was walking behind a woman and four children and a dog. He only had a baby with him. The baby wore a blue bonnet and pink overalls and the man with the drink in his hand couldn't tell if it was a girl or boy. The men said hello to each other, then passed one another. The man with the drink was returning from a short walk to the end of the cove. The man holding the baby looked familiar—not someone he knows personally or knew long ago but a public personality perhaps—an author, politician, TV newsman, someone whose face has been in the news lately, maybe a stage or movie actor. Back again. No men passing, no man on the beach. A quiet cove, except for a lobster boat far out in the water. Dusk, multicolored striped sky. No boat. Plain sky. Just a buoy ringing. No buoy. No sounds. Maybe the wind passing through the trees that line the cove. No wind. Trees along the cove stay. The old boathouse stays. A half-filled glass on a rock in front of the boathouse. The ice in it melted. A slice of lime in it.

The Painter

So the great painter dies. Within minutes of his death the colors disappear from his paintings, the canvases crack and come apart, the frames fall to the floor. Millions of dollars worth of paintings, perhaps a billion dollars worth, are gone. Museum curators summon the police. Private collectors of his work—

No, the painter dies. The great one. Nobody would dispute that. Nothing happens to his paintings after his death. What does change is their value. One painting up for sale that day with an asking price of close to a million dollars, suddenly has an asking price of two million. A private art collector, interviewed on TV that night, says "When I bought this red one ten years ago for a hundred thousand, friends in the know said I paid twice what it was worth. Just a month ago an art dealer offered me five times that amount. Now with his death—not that I don't grieve for him like the rest of us and think, if he was alive and healthy, what he could still do—I could probably get—"

No, the painter dies. The great one. Almost every artist and art expert agrees with that. The paintings he had in his studio will be exhibited this year in a major European museum and then travel to five of the top modern museums in the world before being put on the market. The heirs, to save on paying an estimated hundred million dollars in taxes, have made arrangements with the government where half the paintings—

No, the painter dies. We all know who. The great one. The greatest or second greatest painter in the last fifty years. Certainly one of the five great painters of the century. At least one of the ten great ones in the last hundred years. Definitely one of the ten great ones, of this century, and one of the most influential painters of all time. What modern art movement in the last sixty years hasn't been influenced by him? Maybe some haven't. There have been so many. But five, maybe ten of the major art movements in the last sixty to seventy years have been directly or indirectly influenced by his work. He died in his sleep last night at the age of ninety-one. Ninety-one years old and still painting. The painting he was working on for the last two months was to be one of his largest. Art dealers say the asking price for it, though it's little more than half finished, will be around three million dollars, which will be one of the highest sums paid for a modern painting if it's sold at that price.

No, he's dead. The painter of the century. Or one of them. The day he died—he knew he had little time left, his wife said—he asked her to destroy the painting he was working on. He also asked her to write down his last words. They were "I didn't paint any of the paintings that bear my signature, nor any painting that is said to be mine but doesn't have my signature." All his paintings bear his signature. He then gestured that he wanted to sign his name to the words she wrote down. His son held his writing hand as he wrote his name. Then he said he'd like a glass of his best champagne and some cherries. His wife went for them. By the time she got back he was dead.

No, he died. In his sleep. A peaceful death. Painting he was painting on before he got sleepy and had to be put into bed was of a man sleeping in bed. A dead man, it looked like. Didn't look like an ordinary sleeping man. That's what just about everyone said when the painting was later viewed at an auction house before it was sold for more than three million dollars.

No, he's dead. His paintings aren't. They live on on whatever walls they're on. The colors haven't faded. Nor the themes. They're still alive.

No, they've all faded, colors and themes. The painter for the last week was fading, now he's dead. Died in his sleep. He was drinking champagne at the time. No, can't be.

Dead. The painter. Had a glass of champagne in his hand. He was awake when the glass dropped out of his hand. Or was awake just a moment before the glass dropped out of his hand. His wife, who had her back to him at the time, turned when she heard the glass smash on the floor. Her husband was slumped across the bed, hand dangling just above the floor. She called for her son. "Jose!" He ran into the room. He'd been in bed with the housekeeper in her room a floor above. Two floors above.

No glass broke. He did die while he was in bed. He was put there for a nap, but could have been awake when the accident happened. A painting hanging above the bed, one he did four years ago of his wife and him copulating and which he said he'd never sell for five million dollars, ten million, "all the money from all the countries in the world," fell off its hooks on the wall and hit him on the head. "It probably killed him instantly," the doctor said. The frame alone weighed 200 pounds. The painting doesn't weigh more than a pound or two. "He painted that one thickly," his wife said, "night after night after night for months, and it's one of his largest, so maybe it's three pounds, even four."

No no no. He was killed in an auto accident. He asked his wife the day he died to take him back to the land of his youth. She said he was too frail to go anywhere. He then asked his son to take him there. His son agreed with his mother. "Then I'll get there myself," he said. He tried to get out of bed. They stopped him. He said "I will die of a heart attack tonight if I don't make a quick journey back to the land of my youth." They called the doctor. The doctor said he might be able to survive the trip. So they dressed him and got an ambulance to come. They put him in back of the ambulance on a cot. The ambulance hit a truck three miles from the house and turned over and the painter died. So did the ambulance driver and the attendant in back. His wife broke both arms in the accident. His son was in a car behind them.

No, the painter died in his sleep. In his sleep he was journeying back to the land of his youth. He got out of bed, in his sleep, did half an hour of the same vigorous exercises he used to do thirty years ago, showered and dressed himself, went downstairs, kissed his wife on the lips, patted her backside, kissed his son's forehead, drank a cup of the very strong black coffee he always used to drink in the morning but hadn't been allowed to for ten years, had a large breakfast, more coffee, said "Goodbye, I'll see you both in a few days," went outside, got into his sports car and drove down the hill and past the gatehouse. In his dream a truck hit his car just as he was crossing the border. Just after he crossed the border. Several hours after he'd crossed the border and was driving into the small village of his youth. While he was approaching the farmhouse his family had lived in for more than—

No, in his dream he gets on his horse, after his morning coffee, breakfast, kisses and goodbyes, and rides back to the land of his youth. The journey takes him three days. The horse is the one he had as a youth. He crosses the mountains on it, fords several streams. The border guards of both countries wave him on without asking for his passport. They yell out "Maestro . . . great one." They say "Hail to the liberator of our unconscious . . . emancipator of our imaginations . . . of our dreams." He salutes them, rides for another day to the two-room farmhouse he lived in as a youth. He ducks his head and rides through the front door right up to his old bed. He jumps off the horse, hugs it around the neck, brushes its coat, walks it outside to the grass.

No, he brings grass and water into the house, puts them on the floor, has the horse lie down by the bed. Then the painter gets into his old bed and covers himself up to his neck with his coat. His hair comes back to his bald head. It turns from white to gray to black. His pubic hairs disappear, his chest and back hairs, his wrinkles, illness, clots, most of his scars. He's smaller, shinier, slimmer, solider. His sheet's clean and cool, the bed newer and he has a blanket over him. The horse snores. The young man becomes a boy thinking about becoming a great painter. "I won't be great, I'll just be as good as I can. I'll do things no one else has. No, I'll just paint without thinking what anyone else has done. No, I'll just paint, that's all, and not even think about not thinking of what anyone else has done with paint."

No, the old painter's in bed. In the two-room farmhouse of his youth. His eyes close, he falls asleep. Colors, shapes, patterns, move around in his head. Scenes from his past, from his future. His wife twenty years ago, forty years ago, as his bride. His son as a young man, as a boy, then being born. The painter making love with his wife, with the woman he lived for years with before his wife, with women before that: models, other men's wives, an actress, a princess of a principality, other painters, a young woman he met at a cafe and went to a hotel with, a young woman he met on a train and slept the night in their compartment with, prostitutes in his adopted country, a girl in his native country when he was a schoolboy. In the bed he's in now. His first time, hers. Scenes of his parents working in the fields, his horse drinking from a stream, nudging its dead foal. Sunrise, sunset, nighttime, full moon on top of the chimney of this old farmhouse. "Wake up," his mother says. "Get to work," his father says. "Do you love me?" the young woman on the train as it's pulling into his station. "Do you love me?" his wife says.

"Daddy," his son says. "Papa, dada, fada, ba." Pens, brushes, palettes, tubes of paints. Newspapers calling him a mountebank, defiler, the greatest painter of them all. He tears the newspapers up, pastes them on his canvases, paints over them.

No, the painter's born. We all know who. His mother's legs are open. The doctor says push. Out he comes, brush between his gums, tubes of paint inside his fists. The doctor slaps his behind, cuts the cord. His father gets down on his knees and says "At last, a son," and prays. The painter, no more than eight pounds, starts painting on the soiled sheet. The doctor cleans and dries him, puts a canvas on the floor, the painter crawls on top of it, paints a big circle and then a small circle inside. The outside of the big circle's white, the inside of the small circle's black, the space between the two circles is red. The doctor puts the painter to his mother's breast, blows on the canvas till it's dry, rolls it up, rushes to a gallery with it and sells it for a half a million dollars. It's now worth ten times that. The painter sucks at his mother's breast, nothing comes. He cries, his tears act as a warm compress on her breast, milk comes, he drinks and soon falls asleep. His father goes outside and plants a tree in his son's name. The tree's now ninety-one years old. Once a year till around five years ago the painter returned to the farmhouse to paint that tree. He's kept all of those seventy or so paintings. As a series, art dealers say, the tree paintings could be sold for quarter of a billion dollars. If sold individually the total sale should be around half a billion. The tree has a fence around it, a plaque embedded in the boulder inside the fence which says "This tree was planted on the day of birth of the greatest painter our country has produced in five hundred years. Any defacement of the tree, enclosed area and fence will bring swift prosecution to the full extent of the law." The painter gets out of bed, goes outside, kicks down the fence, pulls an ax out of a tree stump and chops down the tree, has his horse defecate on the boulder and eat the grass in the enclosed area.

When the horse is full it lies down and goes to sleep. The painter lies down, rests his head on the horse's neck and falls asleep. In his sleep he's a newborn child. He floats backwards into the house and up his mother's birth canal. It's dark, it's light, he fingers around for his paintbrush and tubes, the dream explodes.

No, he's an old man riding a paintbrush in the sky. The sky's a clear blue. He seems to be flying around aimlessly. Far below is green farmland, terraced hills, olive orchards, a farmhouse. A boy's sleeping beside a horse. The painter's father is digging a hole. His mother's nursing a baby. His wife's making coffee. His son's playing with the wood toys he carved for him. His infant daughter holds out his eyeglasses to him. She seems to be the only one below who sees him. She drops the glasses and holds up her arms to him. She wants to be picked up. The brush drops out from under him and he floats to earth. The horse stands, shakes itself off, flicks its tail. The painter lands beside it, holds out his arms, someone lifts him and puts him on the horse. He rides to the top of the hill, looks at the brush flying around. His hand reaches up till it's able to snatch the brush out of the sky. He looks around for his paint tubes and a canvas, doesn't see any, and sitting on the horse, starts to paint the sky. Whatever color he wants comes out of the brush. One time he paints the sky five different shades of red, another time a solid gray with a thin yellow line through it, another time it's a combination of fifty different colors. Then he paints it the original blue and flings the brush down the hill.

No, the painter dies. The great one. In the middle of the night. Everyone in the house was asleep. The nurse who was sitting beside him had just fallen asleep. She said she heard a sound in her sleep. We all know what sound. It woke her. Most of the world's newspapers the next day carried the news of his death on the front page.

The Postcard

He goes into the apartment. His wife's waiting for him at the door. "I got this postcard today." She holds it out. He takes it and reads. "Your husband is in love with me, what can I say? Leave him, he doesn't love you. When he makes love with you, it's all sham. That's what he tells me. He pretends to have a good time with you in bed. Oh, all right, maybe he still has a good time with you—at the very end, but every man is like that then. But he has a good time from beginning to end when he's with me in bed. Or on the floor. Or against the wall. Or on the coach. Or even under the coach, and once, I kid you not, in the bathtub. It's me he loves, me he loves making love with, me he wants to be with when he sleeps with you or is just with you. Let him go. Let him be with me. Make him happy, no matter how unhappy it might make you. Are you still reading this? So, what are you going to do? Sincerely, Cecile Strick."

"I never heard of her," he says. "It's some postcard. How can anyone write so small? Must take a special pen or at least a special fine or extra-fine point on a pen. What's this word mean—coach? Couch? Has to be couch. But under the couch? Whoever heard of that? And who has a bathtub so large? I suppose some people have, and that it could be done in just about any size tub. But I've never known a Cecile in my life.

My Aunt Cecile. Forgot her. She's been dead for twenty years—
no, more like twenty-five. I was still in college then."

"You never told me about her."

"Sure I did. I had to. My Uncle Nate used to beat her up.
It's my feeling, but maybe I got the idea from someone in the
family, that he beat her up on the head so much that he was
the cause in some way of her getting brain cancer. That's what
she died of. She was only around fifty. Maybe fifty-five. She
died, actually, more than thirty years ago. I wasn't in college
yet. So maybe she wasn't even fifty. I can't believe she'd be
around eighty now if she had lived. He hit her on the head with
a chair a number of times and once or twice knocked her out.
I remember my father telling me about it. I even remember the
calls he used to get from Cecile that Nate was trying to kill her
again."

"You never told me about him or her."

"Never told you about Uncle Nate? I don't see how I couldn't
have. My father's only brother. Or only one that lived past the
age of five. Whenever we'd see him he used to give us a fifty-
cent coin each. I remember wanting to go over with my brother
and sister just to get that fifty cents. And they were always
shiny—mint condition, almost. As if he got them straight from
the bank and had asked for them to be brand-new. After he
gave us the coin, or just me if I only went with my father, I'd
show it to my mother at home. She was never impressed. They
didn't get along. But poor Cecile. He once tried to throw her
out a window, from maybe ten stories up. They lived on Riverside Drive, around Seventy-Ninth or Eightieth."

"What number?"

"Ninety-Eight."

"That's on Eighty-First, southeast corner. Didn't Bill live there
for a year? Sublet somebody's apartment—Dan Freer's?"

"I think you're right."

"He called today—Bill did. I was going to tell you. He wants you to call him back."

"Did he say about what?"

"Nothing. Just to call back. He sounded loaded. Two o'clock. Loaded. He's never going to be able to finish it."

"Don't worry. He starts it, gets into it, gets loaded for a week or so, and then he finishes it. I've been through it with him before. I'll call after dinner. But Cecile and Nate."

"You're making them up. It's impossible for you to have had an uncle and aunt I never heard of."

"No, I must have told you about them. If you forgot it's because I probably only mentioned them once or twice in five years. Why would I mention them more? I saw Cecile maybe twenty times in my entire life, and only brief visits—maybe once a dinner at their home and they at ours. Nate was a bookie, worked out of his apartment, so we didn't, I think, for that reason—the kids at least—go over there much or stay very long. He usually had, maybe ten hours a day, someone in the kitchen manning the half-dozen phones, and sometimes two to three people working there and in the master bedroom for very big races and sports games. And policemen coming over to get paid off or make bets, and things like that. But I liked going over—and they were only ten or so blocks from us—for the good snacks, and Cecile was always very kind to me, and that half dollar. But when he tried to throw her out the window—well, after that my mother didn't want us to go over there at all. If she disliked him before, she hated and maybe even feared him now. Cecile was two-thirds of the way out the window—head first and face down and he was holding her by her legs and shaking her, shaking her, maybe just to scare her or I don't know what. That's what the doorman saw and told my father and my father told my mother and I overheard. Then some people on the street screamed—or maybe they were in the park, because most of the apartment faced the river—and he pulled

her back in. He also shot her once—after the window incident—
or shot at her, missed, or just grazed her arm—burned her.
Whatever the bullet does. I know she was hurt but not that
hurt. Nate said the wound came from the broken bottle the
bullet smashed, but Cecile always claimed she'd been shot, not
just shot at. Or not, as Nate told my father, that he shot at her
clothes closet ten feet to the left of her, but because he was such
a bad shot, the bullet hit a perfume bottle, I think it was, ten
feet to the left of the closet. Once when we were there I asked
my father to show me where the bullet went. He showed me a
hole in their bedroom wall. The bullet had been dug out but
the hole was still there."

"Maybe he was kidding you."

"About the hole?" She nods. "He did do that. I forget now
where the hole was—by the dresser, the closet, whatever."

"Not that I'm saying there wasn't a shot. But I think it
would have been patched up. By the way, you don't think you
should call Bill now? If he was heading for a big drunk before,
the later you call him, the more incomprehensible he'll probably
be, if he does pick the phone up."

"Maybe I'll wait till tomorrow—around ten; noon, even. Or
see if he calls back tonight. Whatever it is, I know it can hold.
But last time I saw Aunt Cecile was a day or two before she
died. Or a week or two, but she looked so bad—or that's my
memory of it, and I probably only saw her for a few seconds—
that I think of it as a day or two. I don't know why my folks
brought me there. And my mother came this time. I suppose
they thought I was old enough. Fifteen, maybe fourteen. Maybe
they wanted me to play with my cousins Catherine and Ben—
distract them."

"Catherine and Ben? Since when do you have cousins with
those names?"

"Catherine's since died. She got the same brain cancer her
mother had, but the doctors said it wasn't hereditary. 'Coinci-

dence,' they said. I remember the figure of one out of five thousand that two people in the same family would get it. That was about the same as for two people living on the same city block. For a while she was my favorite cousin. We played together a lot, or at least once a month. But hardly ever at her apartment. Almost always at ours or in Riverside or Central Parks. Nate used to beat up his kids too. Ben didn't get it as much. He locked himself in the bathroom or screamed hysterically if he thought he was going to get hit or ran to the neighbors, or just wasn't a target for Nate's violence as much as Catherine and Cecile were. Maybe because those two yelled and fought back. Catherine lost a front tooth to him once. And he hit her head too. Once with a teapot. Picked it up to throw at her and when the water came out of the spout and top—or tea did. Maybe it scalded him and he got even madder because of that, but he hit her head with it. She had to go to the hospital. Had several stitches—maybe thirty. He was a madman. He died by walking into a streetlamp."

"How? He was knocked unconscious, got a head injury—you know, swelling of the brain's membrane from it or a blood clot—and died?"

"It's a mystery. He hit the streetlamp, went down, but it wasn't enough to kill him—just knock him out. In other words, he didn't die from the blow. He died of a heart attack. There was some connection—maybe only a doctor could tell us what it was—but he got the attack while he was lying on the sidewalk. But this is the odd part. A policeman came, tried to revive Nate, searched his pockets for identification, found a whole bunch of bookie slips, and somehow got hold of a policeman friend of his, or something, because in about ten minutes two other policemen showed up at Nate's building, got into his apartment and cleaned out every cent he had stored away there. What's odder is that my father knew some policemen would do that once word got out that Nate had died suddenly on the street.

Apparently every policeman knows that if you're a bookie, and Nate was a very successful one, you've lots of cash stashed away in your home to pay off big winners and such, and also because most of your income is never declared for taxes. In fact, when Ben called my father to tell him Nate had died an hour ago on the street, my father's first response was to tell him to rush right over to Nate's apartment and clear out all the money in two shoeboxes in the bedroom closet. Ben didn't want to. He said that as much as he hated Nate, he still had at least a day's grief and mourning in him for him. But my father told him 'Don't be a moron. I've got grief for him too. But there must be twenty thousand dollars there, and if you don't get it, the cops will.' How'd my father know what the cops would do? He knew lots about city life, that's all. So Ben rushed over to the apartment, but the police were already long gone. He couldn't press charges. For what? Their stealing illegal money? If he did get the money back, the government wouldn't let him keep it anyway. They'd look at all of Nate's reported income over the last five to ten years, and Ben and Catherine, to pay back Nate's owed taxes, would probably have to dig into their inheritance. Ben was also afraid the cops would kill him if he went to the city against them. Nate still left a lot to his kids. Jewelry, gold. But Catherine, married and with a child by then, died a year later from her brain cancer. And Ben's in jail now, my mother says. She saw it in the newspaper a few months ago. Maybe he's out by now—but for running a gambling operation in his home. In fact—well didn't I tell you I met him in an apartment building elevator a year ago?"

"No. I would have remembered. Because it would have been the first time I ever heard of your cousin Ben."

"I don't know why I didn't tell you. I know I wanted to. Reminded myself to tell you, after I met him. Anyway, I hadn't seen him for ten years, probably more. Maybe not since Catherine's funeral. And I heard this guy, running from the lobby, yell 'Hold the elevator. Press the "Door-open" button.' So I pressed the button and in comes Ben. We were both so surprised we even kissed each other's cheeks. I was on my way up to see Hector Lewis. Ben then lived in that building. But according to the newspaper, my mother says, he has another address now, or maybe he gave a phony one to the police. But he was on the top floor, Hector on the eighteenth, and Ben said, as we're going up, 'Guess what I've become in life?' I said 'Well, according to Aunt Ruth you went into the dress business, so I suppose you've become a millionaire.' He said 'A bookie, isn't that amazing? I hated the guy, but I end up doing just what he did, and I think I'm going to do even better than him.' Maybe, after taking a beating in the dress business, he took what experience he'd learned just from watching Nate all those years and started taking book, running gaming tables, which I don't think Nate ever did, and also numbers and stuff, my mother said my cousin Holly told her. Or maybe he was never legit—a word my father like to use—before he became a bookie. I know that as a teenager he was thrown out of a few boarding schools for causing trouble and then in this city got arrested for drunken driving, without a license, but I don't remember hearing of anything worse."

"No wonder you never talked about them. Actually, that's not fair. Because though I can't picture Cecile very well from everything you've said, Catherine seemed very nice."

"She was. And to me, sonofabitch that he was, Nate was still kind of interesting in a way. And look what that poor kid went through—Ben. If I'd had his life as a kid, would I now be much different than he? No matter what—why I also never mentioned Catherine, I don't know. I was never closer to one of my cousins. Then, when she was around fifteen, she got big and fat, and stupid, it seemed, when before she was always curious and perceptive, and I couldn't talk to her about anything except our playing together as kids. Last time I saw her she was so sad she made my cry. She'd lost about a hundred pounds, but it wasn't, and I don't say this to be funny, an improvement. No, forget that. She had no hair. She was wearing a wig. Her speech was slow. She'd gone through operations and one chemotherapy session after the other. My heart bled for her. She acted retarded. But she was so sweet. I don't ever remember her being as sweet as she was then, though she was always a very kind person. Generous. She had about a month to live. In fact, all this took place at one of Cynthia's daughters' weddings. And it's not that she got big and fat and stupid. She got heavy, that was her business, but after everything she went through as a kid, and then was still going through as a fifteen-year-old, you could understand why. She was pretty smart too, in her own way. She was a good businesswoman till she got sick. And whatever I might have suggested, I don't think her sickness was Uncle Nate's doing—hitting her on the head. Or if it was his doing for Cecile's cancer either. I don't know about such things. But what that family's gone through is unbelievable."

"It's still difficult for me to understand how I never heard about any of them. From you, from Ruth. But this card. What's it mean? Who's it from? Who is this Cecile?"

"I don't know. Someone's playing a joke. What's the postmark say? It's this city. Sent yesterday. The mail's faster than I thought. I don't know any Cecile. My Aunt Cecile is the only Cecile I've known. Or that I can remember having known. But certainly no Cecile for years. And this Cecile is talking about today, isn't she? Someone's cracked. Someone's trying to start trouble between us. You're the only person I love and love being in bed with and the only person I go to bed with and there isn't any other woman, and hasn't been since maybe a week or two after I met you, whom I've known in that kind of way."

"I'll accept that," and she tears up the postcard. They kiss. He says "No, a long one, not just a hello, back-from-work kiss." They hug and kiss. Then she says "Like to split a beer?" and he says "Why not?" and follows her into the kitchen.

Windows

Nothing's on his mind. Can't read, doesn't want to sit around the apartment and snack anymore. If he stays here any longer he'll uncork a bottle of wine and drink it down while he looks out the window, stares at the walls, ceiling light fixture and the floor. He gets up to go out. But if I go out, he thinks, where will I go? Take a walk, see what you'll see. Don't stick around here doing nothing, ending up sleepy from all the wine, overstuffed from all the snacks, asleep by seven or eight so up around four or five in the morning and then what'll you do? More staring, eating, drinking. Maybe try the newspaper again.

He sits down, opens the newspaper. Explosion someplace. A woman shot. A woman raped. Two boys find a decomposed body on a beach. Milton Bax wins Endenta Prize. New movies. Spy grabbed. Two dozen pregnant whales run aground. Famous physicist dies of mysterious disease. A young woman crossed the ocean in a canoe. Television listings. Sports. Ads. Juniper Holland's "perfect brownie" recipe. He crumples up the paper, sticks it into the fireplace. Lights the paper, watches it burn. An ash floats through a hole in the fireplace screen and he grabs it in the air. His hand's smudged from the ash. He rubs his hand on his pants. Now his pants are smudged. He brushes his pants till only an indelible spot's left. He sits in the chair. Think about something. Let something just come to mind. Daydream.

He remembers a real event. It was a number of years ago. Three. He was married then and was changing the baby's diapers. Esther. "I peepee," she liked to say, and he or Jill would change her. "If you know when you peepee," he used to say, "then you should try to peepee and kaka into the toilet." "Toilet?" she used to say. "Potty," he used to say. "Potty and toilet, same thing." "Same thing?" she used to say. "Sweetheart, don't repeat everything I say." "Don't repeat?" she used to say. Though it only sounded a little like "Don't repeat." Like her "toilet" only sounded a little like "toilet." "Potty" she could say. "Dough repee," she used to say. "Toyet. Same sin." She didn't peepee into the toilet till she was three. People said that was very late. He and his wife didn't mind her not using the toilet till then. Some things one gets used to. And he liked changing her most times. The softness of the diapers, patting her crotch and bottom with a warm washrag, drying her, pinning the diapers on her, the rubber pants, the long pants or stretchies or shorts. She would be on her back on the changing board and he would be sitting in front of her on the same bed and he would often lean over and kiss her forehead or the top of her head or her cheek. Sometimes he'd say "Kiss daddy," and she'd kiss his cheek. Then he'd finish dressing her, if he hadn't already finished, and stand her up on the floor or just lift her off the board and put her into or back into bed.

But he was changing her, he remembers, when the phone rang. He looks at his hand. Still a little dirt. He picks at it with his fingernail, then spits into a handkerchief and rubs it into his hand till the spot's gone. It's not that I mind dirt, he thinks. He smells his hand. It smells from spit, but that'll go away quickly enough. And an ash really isn't dirt. I could, in fact, almost any other day, walk around with my hand smudged like that or even worse. Not the whole hand smudged, but a much larger spot than there was. Anyway: walk around or just stay here without paying any attention to the smudge till it disappeared through nothing I consciously did.

He turns around and looks out the window. About fifteen feet from his window are two windows in a brick wall. Above the wall—his apartment and the apartment or apartments he's looking at are on the top floors of their buildings—is some gray sky. Maybe I should stare at that slit of sky till something passes in it. A bird, helicopter, sheet of newspaper, a plane. Rain, even. Stare till it rains. It can't snow. Not the season for it. What else could be in the sky that might pass, drop, stay there awhile, float by? A cloud, of course. Hailstones would be unlikely. A balloon. On the other side of the building he's looking at is a street. Someone could walk on it holding a balloon. The balloon could be released, accidentally, intentionally, and float past that slit of sky he's looking at. He looks at that sky for around two more minutes, tells himself to look at it another minute and if nothing passes in it, to stop. He looks at it another minute. Nothing passes. He faces forward, rests his head back against the chair, remembers.

The phone rang. He yelled something like "Jill, would you get it?—I'm changing the baby." She yelled she would and ran to her studio from wherever she was and picked up the phone. "Oh Randi," she said, "hi," and that's all he remembers hearing from that phone call. That was all he heard. Because he remembers that maybe an hour later he thought about why he hadn't heard more of the phone conversation than just "Oh Randi, hi," and decided it was because she must have started speaking very low after that or else had shut the door. He never asked her about it, though once or twice had wanted to. But she came into the baby's room a few minutes later, while he was on the floor putting away Esther's books and toys and Esther was sitting on the floor trying to string beads, and looked very sad. She was very sad, but when she came into the room, or rather, stood inside the door with her shoulder against the jamb, as if, if she didn't lean against it she wouldn't be able to stand, all he could tell was that she looked very sad. What he thought then was that she was sad because of something she'd learned over the phone or something that had happened to her since she put the phone down. Because, he thought, what could Randi have told her that made her look so sad? And how come she didn't let him speak to Randi? She was his niece. They were quite close. Maybe Randi had called to tell him something about his sister, but something so terrible that she was now relieved she wouldn't have to be the one to tell him. "What is it," he said, "something wrong?" She nodded. She brought her hand to her mouth.

He hears a plane, turns around to that slit of sky but doesn't see anything. Then he sees it for a couple of seconds. Flying west. A jumbo jet. It could be going to any number of places. California, Tahiti, Japan. It could be going, eventually, east. If it is, it'll soon turn around. But chances are much better, not that he really knows what he's talking about, that it's going west, or west now but north or south soon. He looks at the two windows. He's never seen anyone in the right one. The shade's always down. Never even seen the room. He's seen artificial light behind the shade. In the evening, very late, maybe five or six times. But he's never seen the shade raised even an inch from the sill in the year and two months he's lived here. The fourteen months since Jill asked him to leave their apartment, which he did and got this apartment that same day. In the other window—it's much smaller—he's seen a woman showering maybe fifteen times. Showering or just shampooing, if one doesn't always shower, meaning clean one's body, which he's never seen her do, except for her face and neck, when one shampoos. He wonders if the shaded window is part of the same apartment as that bathroom. The bathroom door is at the end of the left wall. If it was in the right wall, then the bathroom would have to lead to the shaded room. Though maybe the shaded room is a hallway in that apartment or a public hallway in that building. If he steps up to his window he can see four windows on the same floor to the right of the shaded window, two with blinds, two with shades, all opened or closed or lit or unlit at various times of the day, but none, except for the one next to the shaded window and there only a little, can he see inside. Not the right angle or too far away. But a public hallway wouldn't have a shaded window. Makes no sense. For the last two months the bathroom window has had a shade on it. Almost to the sill. Possibly because she caught him watching her showering several times. Sometimes it was by accident. He'd be slumped below the top of the padded chair when he'd hear a shower go on, look around or above the chair and see her showering. Or he'd enter his apartment, shut the door and see her showering. Hear and see at the same time sometimes. The shower part of her bathtub is right by the bathroom window. For a while at night when he came home he wouldn't turn on his apartment light till he found out if she was showering or not. If she was, he'd watch her in the dark till she left the bathroom or put her bathrobe on. If she only put on her underpants or bra, he'd continue to watch her till she left the room. If she put both underclothes on, he'd crawl away from the window to one of the lights, turn it on and stand and go about the apartment as if he just came home. But he only caught her showering once in the eight or so times when he came home and went through this routine, so he gave it up. She's a woman of about thirty-five, somewhat plump, somewhat pretty, who spends a great deal of time lathering her long dark hair. Sometimes he's seen her entirely covered with lather, which would start at her hair and slide down on all sides and sometimes in large clumps to the rest of her body, or the parts of her body he could see above the bathtub rim. He's gotten quite excited sometimes when he's seen her showering or drying herself and then putting on her underclothes. Once when she saw him looking at her while he was standing in the middle of the room and pretending to flip through a magazine, she slammed the window down and pulled the single shower curtain around her where he couldn't see her showering anymore, not that he would have been able to see much through the smoked glass. Once when it was night and he was reading in this chair, he heard her singing in the shower. He doesn't know if he had been so absorbed in the book that he had missed the shower going on, or else if the shower and singing had started at the same time. Anyway, he stood up, with his back to her put the book on the chair, shut the light, opened his door, slammed it, crawled to the far right corner of the window and raised his head just above the sill to watch her. By the time she was drying herself while standing in the tub, he had his pants down and his handkerchief out. He wonders about a woman who'd shower in front of an open window, one that faces another open window, especially one in which she must have known a man had caught or watched her showering several times. Maybe she has a let-him-look attitude about it, all he's seeing is a body, one not much different than any other woman's body her age, and if it does anything to him, it has nothing to do with her. Or maybe she liked showering in front of him, showing off her body, so to speak, the pleasure it might give him, let's say, maybe even showering more times than she normally would because he was there, but then felt the situation had possibilities or ramifications she hadn't thought about, so she stopped. He can't see her toilet or sink from his window. They must be on the right side of the bathroom.

Jill took her hand away from her mouth. He forgets what Esther was doing at the time. She was probably just lying peacefully or squirming a little but on her back. But why'd he pick this particular memory? It's the one that came to him, that's all. It could have been one of any number of memories that came to him when he just sat back and let things enter his head. The time his mother died. (He was in the hospital room.) The time

Esther was born. (He was in the delivery room.) The time he and Jill got married. (It was in the living room of the apartment she and Esther now live in.) The time he learned his brother's plane had disappeared. (He was in his sister's living room.) The time Jill ran into the bathroom with her nightgown on fire. (He was on the toilet. She had said from the kitchen only a half-minute before "Do you smell gas?" He had said "No, why—you mean real gas? Do you?") The time Jill accepted his marriage proposal. (He was on his knees in her living room, his arms around her legs, crying, while she was rubbing his head with one hand and with the other trying to get him to stand.) The time an ice cream popsicle stuck to the entire top of his tongue. (He was standing on a busy street corner, pointing to his mouth and gagging. The ice cream vendor got in his truck and drove off. A man said "Don't pull on it, kid. It's the dry ice it was packed in. Pull on it and you'll take off half your tongue. Just let it melt a few minutes and it'll come off on its own.") The time Esther fell, though it actually seemed she had flown, down a flight of stairs. (They were in the summer cottage they rented and which Jill still rents. He was in the main room, working at his desk. Something made him look to his left and he saw her flying headfirst down the stairs. The staircase was in the hallway around twenty feet away, but he missed catching her by just a couple of inches at the bottom of the stairs. He doesn't see how that was possible. He must have seen her on one of the top steps, about to fall, and jumped out of his chair and ran to the stairs.) The time they took Esther to the hospital. (They were in their car, minutes after he'd missed catching her at the bottom of the stairs. He was driving. Esther was in Jill's lap in the rear seat, a compress on her nose, towels around her bleeding head. A rabbit jumped across the road and he swerved but hit it. The rabbit flew over the car and landed about fifty feet behind them. He'd hit it while it was in midair. Jill screamed. Esther was unconscious.) The time they waited while the doctors and nurses treated Esther. (It was outside the hospital examination room. They thought she was going to die. One of the doctors had said a few minutes before "I don't know if you know it, but she may die." Jill said "Listen, you imbecile. I know we were negligent, but now's the stupidest time in the world to remind us." The doctor said he didn't mean it that way. Jill said "You did too." Carl pulled her into him, said "Don't argue, don't bother, don't worry, it'll all turn out all right. It's got to be all right. I'll go crazy if she dies.") The time they buried his father. (Cemetery.) His mother. (Same cemetery.) The time he came home from summer camp and his parents said they'd given away his dog.

Jill said to him "—died." He said "Who?" "—Kahn." "What? I'm not hearing you for some reason. Who?" "Gretta Kahn. Gretta Kahn. She died two days ago, Monday." "Oh Jesus, that can't be. It can't. What are you talking about? That was Randi on the phone, right? So what's she got to do with Gretta?" "Not your niece, Randi. Gretta's oldest son, Randy. He called from Charleston. Gretta died in San Diego. A massive heart attack, he said. She was visiting Mona. And because he knew she was such a good friend of ours—" "Her daughter?" "Mona, her daughter and Randy's sister, yes. They're having the funeral in San Diego—something about it's easier to, not the expense—and just wanted us to have the option of coming. I told him I didn't think we could. I was right, wasn't I?" "Come on," he said, "she was too healthy. Anyone but her. Besides, it's too ridiculous. For it was just around this time of year last year—" "That's right. It's like a medical prophecy come true, except it's the reverse of what frequently is supposed to happen in that frequently it's the husband who dies a year after his wife." He remembers she cried, they talked a lot about Gretta that night, neither of them slept well, and this went on for two or three days. She was one of their best friends. And of their best friends, she was just about the nicest of them and the one they loved most. Or else it seemed that way at the time. Was it so? He thinks it was, and if it wasn't, then she came as close as anyone at the time to being the nicest of their best friends and the one they loved the most. They didn't have many friends that both of them considered their best friends. He had best friends, she did. A few they shared. Or he had several fairly good friends, she had several very good friends, and a few of her very good friends he considered fairly good friends of his. What's he talking about? Gretta was a very good close friend of them both. They talked about deep serious things together, all three of them or just when he or Jill was with her. Sometimes. Sometimes they just had a good time together, when not a serious subject or mood came up. Jill and he didn't go to Gretta for advice, either separately or together, and she never came to either of them for it, but when they were with one another, separately or together, they often talked about the most important things in their lives, past or present, including what was bothering them most. When he or Jill were alone with Gretta they also occasionally talked about their respective spouses, something they didn't do with Gretta's husband Ike and Ike didn't do with them, talk personally about Gretta or about anything deep or serious that might interest either of them, though they still considered him to be one of their dearest friends, because he was so generous and warm and Gretta's husband, though maybe not one of their closest. He remembers trying to bring Gretta back then in his thoughts. Three years ago. He remembers that a day or so after Gretta died he said to Jill when the phone was ringing "Maybe that's Randy again, saying it was only a joke and Gretta isn't dead." He remembers Jill saying "That's crazy" or "too bizarre for me." "I know that was crazy or too bizarre," he remembers saying after he or she finished talking to whomever it was on the phone, "what I said about Gretta before, but it was what I wished most. That it had been a joke. To lose Ike one year, Gretta the next? To lose them both? All a joke. For

Randy or Mona or whatever the other son's name is—Gene—
to say on the phone 'Gretta and Ike are alive. They said they'll
explain everything when they get to New York and see you
all.' " He remembers lying in bed the next few days thinking of
the various ways she could be alive. That it was a seizure of
some kind where she appeared dead but wasn't. Or she had
been dead but was revived. Where they'd get a letter from Gretta
the next day or so explaining why Randy gave Jill that message
and why she had to send this letter instead of making a phone
call. That it was a bet. That it was part of a plot. That it was
a chain of almost inconceivable false and incompetent medical
reports from hospital to doctor to Gretta's children. It took him
a while to get used to her death.

He hears a shower turned on behind him. He turns around.
The shade's down, woman's singing. Both their windows are
open. The weather's been gray and unseasonably cool the last
few days but has warmed up in the last hour and the sun's now
out. He looks at the sky. He recognizes the melody she's singing
but can't make out the words. He shuts his eyes and listens.
She's singing in French, but he's almost sure the song's American. She has a sweet voice. Professional, almost. For all he knows
about singing voices, professional. Dulcet was the word Jill used
for a voice this sweet. Jill knew about voices. She listened to
opera, lieder and madrigals a few hours a day, once wanted to
be an opera singer, sang in several languages in the shower
sometimes but would never do it with the window open or so
loud. "Sweeter than sweet," she said, "is when you use 'dulcet,'
or at least when I use it." He doesn't know if he'd recognize
this woman if he saw her on the street. For one thing, it's been
a long time since he's seen her in the shower. If he saw her and
recognized her would he introduce himself? He doubts it. Of
course not. Would she recognize him if she saw him? He doubts
it. Maybe she would. Maybe she's already seen him on the street
and recognized him several times while all to some of those times

he might have looked straight at her but didn't recognize her. He wouldn't mind meeting her. He knows no woman to go out with. He hasn't been to bed with a woman since Jill, though he has been out with a number of them but never more than once or twice each. The third or fourth time is when you often get to go to bed together. He wonders if he should call Jill. He'd ask how she is. She'd say fine, probably, but why did he call? "To find out how you are and to find out, of course—how could you even ask that?—how Esther is." "You spoke to Esther this morning," she could say, "you'll see her this weekend. She's having her supper now." It's around that time. He looks at his wrist. His watch isn't on it. Where'd he leave it? This could lead to a minute or two of panic. Watch, pen and wallet, all quite valuable when one considers the wallet's contents, and all given to him by Jill. Sentimental value then? Not only. But when they're out of his pockets and off his wrist, he likes to keep them together. The dresser. He goes into the bathroom, sees the three of them and his checkbook and keys on top of the dresser, looks at the watch. He should buy a clock. A small one, that doesn't tick. It's five after six. Just around the time she'd be eating. He used to like feeding her. "Baby eat meat," she used to say. "Baby eat corn and peas, no beans," though she used to pronounce them "con and peats." Used to like putting the bib on her, making sure her hands were clean and if they weren't, washing them with a little warm water on a dish towel and drying them with the towel's other end. Now she feeds and washes herself, though sometimes when she insists he lets her eat with slightly dirty hands. Now she tucks the napkin into her shirt or spreads it out on her lap, though sometimes he lets her use her sleeve. He used to like feeding her spoonfuls and forkfuls of food, touching the cereal with his tongue before he gave it to her to make sure it wasn't hot. Squeezing orange juice for her almost every morning, every so often squeezing quarter of a grapefruit to add to the glass. He was usually the first up. Around six. Esther around seven. Jill around eight. Putting her to bed—he liked that too. Bathing her first, though the one who bathed her usually wasn't the one who then read to her and put her to bed. And after he washed her but while she was still playing with her water toys or the soap in the tub, massaging and brushing and flossing his teeth and gums and then applying that sodium bicarb-peroxide paste. He didn't like giving her shampoos. Liked rubbing her back to get her to sleep. Making love with his wife while the baby slept in the same room. She was always so receptive. His wife was. They loved each other, and he thinks the baby, as much as a one-to-two-year-old could, loved him then too. What went wrong? Why did it have to go wrong? Were there several or many things wrong or just one main one? He still loves Jill but she no longer loves him. That's what she's said so that's what he has to believe. He should go out. Take a walk, see what he sees. Not a movie. Maybe step in for coffee someplace, regular or espress. Maybe a beer. No beer. He doesn't like drinking in bars alone. Doesn't like eating out alone. Coffee in some stand-up place or on a coffee shop stool is still okay.

The shower's turned off. The singing's stopped. She's probably drying herself but she could also be shaving her underarms or legs. Saw both of those once or twice too. Today she left the shade up a couple of inches, but it's not dark enough outside yet to look. Not dark at all. Anyway, he shouldn't be sneaking looks. Maybe he should go out to buy a men's magazine. One with naked women, but which still has serious articles and maybe serious fiction in it. Photos showing everything, but of women alone or together rather than with naked men. He doesn't like to buy that kind of magazine, give a clerk money and sometimes have to get change back for it, walk home with it rolled up if he doesn't have an envelope or newspaper to put it in, or have it around the apartment. But about every three to four months, maybe two to three months is a closer estimation, he buys one, uses it in his own way, then tears it up after a couple of days and sticks the pieces deep into a garbage bag, makes sure they're covered with garbage, and drops the bag in one of the trash cans in front of his building. But he doesn't want to go out just to buy one of those magazines, though he wishes now he hadn't torn up the last one he bought.

He turns around and looks at the sky. Go out. See what's out there. Call Jill. Ask to speak to Esther. Go to a movie. Go to a bar. Go to a bookstore and buy a book whatever it costs. For the first time in your life, find a book you want very much to read but any other time you'd think way too expensive for you. If you haven't the cash, write a check. If they won't take a check, ask them to put the book aside, leave a deposit for it, go back to the apartment, and next day, or even tonight, if the store's still open and not too far away, get that book. Or just walk along the street. Walk to walk. Walk for exercise. For fresh air. To tire yourself out. Walk all the way downtown. Through the theater district. Past the Village to Lower Broadway. Go to several bookstores and bars and then cab home. Or call Jill and say you're sad and lonely and want to come back to her. "I want us to live as a family again," say. "I love you," say. "I love Esther. It's not that I can't live without you. It's that I don't want to. Living alone's killing me in a way. I sneak looks at the bathroom window across from my apartment. A woman showers there and I want to see her nude. I have seen her nude, she's bought a shade just to keep me from seeing her nude, but I often quickly turn my head to her window hoping the shade's up and she's standing there nude. I have these absurd fantasies about meeting her on the street and going to bed with her. I think about buying those awful men's magazines just to use the photos of naked women in them to alleviate my excitedness. My sexual frustration. My pent-up whatever it is that keeps getting more pent-up every day. I have bought those magazines, maybe every other month. I thought of Gretta today.

I think of her a lot. Not in a sexual way. I'm sorry I linked those two subjects up like that. One coming after the other. Gretta and sex. Or rather those magazines and Gretta. But I think of her a lot. Those were good days then, the time when we knew her and she died. I mean, we were sad for her. It crippled us for a while. But we were happy with one another then, the time when we knew her and a little after the time she died. The two of us and the three of us, meaning the two of us when that's all there was of us and then with Esther, and you can't say we weren't. I know I had a bad temper. You can't say we weren't happy then. I know I was impossibly moody at times. But I'm getting to understand the reasons why I had those sudden swings of mood and also how to prevent them and I doubt I'll ever get like that again or at least as much." Call and say all that. Or walk or take a cab acrosstown and ring her bell from the lobby and ask to come up. Then say it to her or as much as you think she can take for one time.

A plane's overhead. He looks out the window. The plane passes but not in the part of the sky he's able to see. Jill has a lover now. She's in love. They'll probably get married. That's what she's said. He's met him. Seems like a decent fellow. And tall, handsome, rugged, smart. Esther likes him too. Loves him in a little girl's way, Jill's said. He's wonderful and attentive and devoted to both of them, Jill's said, and when the three of them are together they get along exceptionally well. Go outside. Take that walk. Exhaust yourself walking so you'll sleep eight to ten hours straight. Have an exotic coffee outside, have brandies and beer, have a good dinner outside and then buy a book, or buy it before you have dinner, you never would have bought for yourself before and come home. He gets up to go. He hears a shade snapped up. Bathroom's? He looks at his ceiling, floor, slowly turns around to look at that woman's bathroom. It's the shaded room's shade that's up. It must have snapped up by accident. No one seems to be in the room. It's unlit. He goes up to his window and sees a mirror at the end of that room reflecting his building's roof and the light from the sky above it. Someone goes over to the mirror and looks into it. From behind it looks like Gretta. That's the way she looked from behind. He saw her walking away from him, from them, down her road, picking a blossom off a tree, berries off a bush, going into rooms, working in her kitchen, cooking there, putting away dishes there, putting seeds into the bird feeders around her house, snapping pictures, serving hors d'oeuvres, many times. Kind of short, round, hair like that. Shape like that. Way she's fussing with her hair now like that. Then a man, both are fully dressed, comes into view and walks up behind her and hugs her while they both look into the mirror, the man looking over her shoulder. He can't see their faces in the mirror. Their images are entirely blocked by their standing in front of the mirror. Then they turn around and come up to the window, the man with his hand on her shoulder. It's Ike and Gretta. Ike raises his hand to pull the shade down and sees him looking at them. Ike points to him, they stare at him. Gretta seems shocked, Ike amused. He says "Gretta, Ike, oh God, this is too wonderful. Tell me what apartment you're in and I'll run right over. I'm so lonely. I was till I saw you. On and off, I mean, and sad—you can't believe how much—on and off too. Jill and I are divorced. She's going to remarry, while I love her as much as I ever did. That was a lot, remember? but that's not news. Esther's just great. A truly exemplary child. Intelligent, beautiful, generous, precious, good; a real dear. We missed you so. We were devastated by your deaths. The untrue news of them, rather, for here you are. We both loved you so. Love you so, love you, and I know I can still speak for Jill on this. Seeing you now is the best thing that's happened to me in a year. In two, in three. Or come over here. I'm in number nine, apartment 5D. But I'll run over to your place because I know I can get there faster than you could here. Or maybe, with this shade business of Ike's—raising his hand to pull it down, it seemed like—and the look that was on both your faces, you had something else in mind and want me to wait here a half-hour or so. You can hear me through your closed window, can't you?"

He didn't go over to his window. He stood almost at the other end of his room, looking out his window from there. Shade on the window of the once shaded room did snap up, bathroom shade stayed down. He didn't see a mirror in that room. If there is one, and in the place he said there was, then he imagined it before he saw it, for so far he's been too far away from that room to see anything inside. The room's unlit, though. That he can see from where he stands. He goes over to his window and looks inside that room. There's a double bed, made, in there. A night table beside it. A lamp on the table. Ashtray next to the lamp. Radio beside the ashtray. Cup in a saucer on top of the radio. That's all he can see in the room. Spoon in the saucer. Maybe a crack in the wall but nothing's hanging on the part of the wall he can see. What will the tenant think when he or she, if there's only one, sees the shade up? That it snapped up on its own? That a stranger was in the room and let it up? But how will she or he pull it down? Will he or she allow him- or herself to be seen from a window across from that building? It's worth waiting for. Just to see the reaction of that person, if it can be seen, when she or he sees the shade up, and what kind of person lives there.

He moves the chair from the left side of his window to the right. He turns the chair around to the window and pushes it within inches of the window. He opens a bottle of wine, sits in the chair and drinks while he faces at an angle the now unshaded room. The day gets darker. He can see a big chunk of the sky from here. His phone hasn't rung, when he's been in his apartment, for almost two days. Stars come out. Two, three, then a few of them. The bathroom window shade stays down. The light in the bathroom goes on and off a few times in the next two hours. Twice it stayed on for only a few seconds, once for almost a half-hour. He finishes three-quarters of the bottle of wine, has to pee. It's now night. Many stars are out. He can see the moon's light but not the moon. The bathroom light hasn't been turned on for about an hour. If the bathroom is part of the same apartment as the bedroom, he's sure the woman who likes to shower would have walked into the bedroom by now. Or at least a door would have opened from the bathroom or some other part of the apartment—a hallway—into the bedroom and let some light into it by now. But no light's come in. A little light from the moon perhaps. But now the bedroom's almost black. He can't see anything inside it. He finishes off the bottle. Now he really has to go to the bathroom or he'll have to do it in his pants right here. Maybe into the bottle, but that would end up being a mess. He tries to hold it in. He doesn't want to miss that person or persons, if there is more than one person living in that apartment containing that room, discovering the shade up and then pulling it down. And he's certain it'll be pulled down. But he can't hold it in anymore and runs to the bathroom. He takes his watch off the dresser while he's there. The shade's still up and the bedroom's still dark when he gets back. An hour later he has to go to the bathroom again. He runs to it, pees, runs to the kitchen and gets a beer out of the refrigerator, runs back to the chair. Nothing's changed in that room. He opens the beer, sips, puts it down, wakes up in the chair and finds the shade down but the room still dark. He doesn't know how long he's been sleeping in the chair. He should take a walk. He looks at his watch. He can't make out the luminescent numerals and hands. He squints. Still can't make them out. He gets up and turns on the side table light. It's past two. That's hard to believe, he thinks. He should go to sleep. Maybe have a bite to eat from the food in the refrigerator and a slice of bread and then go to sleep. No, just take off your clothes, pull out the bed and go to sleep.

A Friend's Death

He gets a disease and suffers from it and dies. Before that Kirt visits him in the hospital several times. Once when Chris went in for tests to see what was giving him so much pain. Other times when he was in the hospital suffering from the disease the tests showed he had, and then the last time the day before he died. Kirt also visited him at home between the times he was in the hospital and also met him at a coffee shop once, but Chris got so sick there that Kirt had to take him to the hospital.

Chris was sitting up in bed the first time Kirt saw him in the hospital. He said "I know I'm very sick, even if they don't know what I got yet. But it's not in the head. Meaning it's not in my mind, because the truth is I think what I got's going to spread to my head. But that's not here nor there now. Right now I know I'm very sick in the liver, in the stomach—one of those organs around there and maybe a couple of them. I know it's going to kill me but I don't know when. I'm almost sure I won't be around in a year or so, and my real feeling is I won't last six months."

Kirt told him "The worst thing you can do is diagnose yourself. That's what we have doctors and pathologists and people like that for. Ninety percent of the time the patient's wrong in his self-diagnosis. What I've heard is that about sixty to seventy

173

percent of the time the results from the tests turn out to be much better than what the patient predicted they'd be and that about twenty percent of the time the results aren't as bad as the patient thought. It's fear that makes you think it's worse than it is. Just go through the tests, try not to worry about anything, don't build things way out of proportion, think you're going to get well and feel better and that what you have isn't so bad and in fact is nothing, and your chances of something not being wrong with you will greatly improve. It has something to do with the body's chemistry, I heard, but don't ask me to explain what exactly that is or how it works. All I know is that if you think positively about your health, you're already a few percentage points—maybe even ten to fifteen percentage points—better off than if you think the worst about your physical condition. And eat well, do what the hospital people say, sleep well—all of it adds a percentage point or two to your getting better and staying healthy from then on."

"No," Chris said. "I know it's bad, I know it's terminal, and I can't face it. Maybe if I had had years and years to get used to it, but coming so suddenly, I just don't have the courage to die."

The next time Kirt saw him was at Chris's home. He said to Kirt "Well, I got the test results from the doctor this week and I turned out to be absolutely right. What I have is fatal. The word is that people with my disease and in the form it's taken and rapid way it's progressed, usually don't last a year. So, unless a miraculous cure's discovered in the next few months—and the researchers working on it aren't even close to one—I'm on my way out for sure. I can't face it. I'll never adjust to it. I'm going to get crazier and crazier in the head because of it. Long suffering and then death are the two things I fear most. What should I do? Tell me, you're smart—what should I do?"

"Think that everything's going to be all right, and I mean that," Kirt said. "Think that the doctors, for all they know, could be wrong too. Think that they'll find that the most important test result that came back was wrong. Or that one of the treatments they give you will work a hundred percent. Or that they will discover a miracle cure for your disease in the next few months and one that will take effect immediately on you. Listen. Even if you told me now that only five percent of those who have your disease survive after a year, think that you'd be one of those five percent. You will live and eventually be healthy, believe me. I know it in my bones and everywhere else inside of me that you're going to pull through, and you have to believe that too."

Chris was admitted to the hospital a week later. When Kirt saw him there, Chris was suffering terribly. "Nothing they give me stops the pain," he said. "The experimental painkiller that was giving me some relief apparently has hurt more people than it's helped, so they took me off it for the time being till they test it out some more. I can't sleep, I can't eat. They're putting me on I.V. Please don't tell me I'm going to get better. I've done nothing the past few months but get worse. If I'm going through this much pain without anything much to alleviate it, what should I expect to come next? I'm also as scared as I ever was not only of dying but of being dead. My brother, who to him spent a considerable sum to fly here, couldn't take my complaining and morbid talk anymore and flew back to France. You're in charge of running things for me if you'll do it. These are my instructions: I want to be kept alive no matter what. Life support systems and experimental drugs and treatments, if the more proven stuff doesn't work, all the way. In the end, anything they've never tried before but want to start on someone, give it a shot on me. Only after I'm flat and out dead do I want the systems turned off. I've written all this down and my last wish to you is to carry them out."

Kirt said "Believe me, it'll never come close to being that bad. I spoke to the doctor in charge on this floor and she's very hopeful the present treatments will work on you and that a complete cure will be found in a year or two. And she swears nobody's said to you that your condition is terminal."

"They haven't because I told them not to, but I know it is but don't want to know for sure. That'll make it even worse for me in the head. But if they did tell you there was no chance in the world for me, and I'm sure they have, you wouldn't tell me, right? Because you know I don't want to know, and besides that, your philosophy is to keep the patient thinking positively. And how could I think positively if the most positive person I know tells me I'm going to die in a few months? But you will carry out my instructions, won't you?"

"They won't be necessary, but I'll do anything you want."

In one of Kirt's next visits to the hospital, Chris was lying on his back in bed. Tubes were in him, he could barely speak. He paused after every few words and most of the time Kirt had to strain to hear him. He did manage to say in one spurt "I told you so, didn't I? On a stack of bibles: it's everything I didn't want." It took him about a half-hour to say "Don't bury me belowground. You mustn't. A steel casket, thoroughly sealed. If steel isn't the most airtight and impenetrable casket going, then get what is. I want nothing coming into my casket ever, or at least while my body's still relatively intact. I want to dry up to almost nothing before anything's able to get inside. Maybe in a hundred years, maybe in two. Tell my brother that when he returns for the funeral. Insist. I've signed and given to my lawyer a power of attorney putting you in total charge of whatever there might be of my estate and all the funeral arrangements and things once I'm gone. But my brother might fight it, and being my only blood relative and a battler when he sees what he thinks is waste, he might win. You've my original instructions?"

Kirt kissed him on the forehead.

"Disease, you'll get my disease."

"Nonsense," and he patted Chris's hand.

"I'll get better, yes? Oh yes, I'll get better. I'll be jumping around like a jumping jack in a few days."

"I wish you would get better. And you can, you know. People have come back healthy and strong from the most extreme states of sickness and lack of strength, not that your condition has gone that far."

"The doctors don't say that to you about me, do they? No, don't tell me what they say."

Kirt saw him in the hospital the day before he died. Chris couldn't speak. He wanted to write something to Kirt, but couldn't hold the pen. When Kirt came back from a snack in the hospital cafeteria, Chris was in a coma. He never came out of it. His brother was there. He spoke to Kirt in French, Kirt said he couldn't understand but a few words, his brother cried in his arms. "The poor man," his brother said in French. "So young. So terrible. So unnecessary."

The next day the brother had someone call Kirt to tell him in English that Chris had died. There wasn't any problem with the brother over money or the instructions or anything like that, and Chris was buried inside a steel vault aboveground.

Kirt went to the aboveground burial site a year later. Rented a car and went alone. He'd been thinking a lot about Chris the last week, hadn't been to the site since the burial, and wanted to pay his respects and see if the vault was being looked after. He stood in the corridor in front of Chris's vault. It was one of about three hundred vaults in this wall of the building, and he had passed several similar corridors to get to it. No plaque was on Chris's vault. The only way to identify it was the vault's number. Chris hadn't left instructions for a plaque or memorial of any kind. Kirt wrote the brother about it a week after the funeral, the brother wrote back that he'd get one installed with Chris's name, birthplace and dates, but that seemed to be the end of it. Chris had no relatives in this country. Kirt had been his one friend for years. His former wife and stepchildren wouldn't see him in the hospital, when Kirt called them to say how sick Chris was, or come to the funeral. The only other attender at the funeral besides the brother and Kirt was Chris's business partner, someone Chris distrusted and who he said distrusted him. The woman friend he had for two years, but split up with a month before he got sick, said she'd like to visit Chris in the hospital, and when Kirt called her again, would like to come to the funeral, but she was working on a project for her firm that was tying her down day and night. Chris's lawyer was out of town the day of the funeral. His personal physician said he never went to the funeral of one of his patients unless the patient happened to be a relative or close friend. Several people Chris had done business with said they were too busy or unwell to come. Chris's landlady said he was a good tenant, always paid his rent on time, never caused a fuss, but she hardly knew him. Kirt had called her to say Chris had died and if she'd like to attend his funeral. He had wanted more people to be there other than Chris's partner and brother and he. Only Kirt and the brother were at the burial, other than for the minister and the workers who put the casket into the vault. Half of Chris's estate, minus the funeral and burial expenses and whatever bills and debts Chris had, went to his brother and the other half was split between his university and the foundation doing research on his disease. All of this was stipulated in his will.

Kirt wrote a poem the night before and read it standing very close to the vault. " 'Kirt I miss you, Kirt I. . . . ' Oh my God," he said, "I put in my own name." He crossed out his name, wrote in Chris's, and read from the poem again. " 'Chris I miss you, Chris I kiss you. I'm sorry, sorry, a dozen poems, a hundred plaintive groans, can never say how much. You were a relatively successful but very lonely man. I wouldn't want your success if such loneliness depended on it, and I doubt you wanted it that way too. I wish we had leveled with one another more. The aftermath is always filled with regrets, but what are we going to do? Patterns, grooves, et cetera. I was proud to be your friend. Obviously, I can't write poetry for the life of me, but right now I feel I can only say what I have to this way. Life has been a dark place for me too without you. I didn't know how good a friend I had till you were gone. I think I've contradicted myself somewhere there, but so what? I wish more people had come to your funeral. It might have meant there was a little more happiness in your life than I'm convinced there was. What else can I say? Tomorrow I will sit on a bench there, if there's one, and be silent for a minute after I read you this poem, and then go. I'll be back. There is a lack in my life as there was in yours.' "

He tore up the poem, stuck the pieces into his jacket pocket. There were two benches nearby but he didn't sit. He put his hands in front of his face, closed his eyes, leaned his head against Chris's vault, cried, remained still like that for several minutes after he cried, left.

As he was walking to the parking lot, a man he had never seen before came alongside him and said "I was standing several graves, or whatever you want to call those things, over from you when you were inside before. I don't mean to intervene, but we seem to be walking in the same direction to lot B. That must have been one hell of a person you visited just now. One really wonderful person. My condolences, no matter how long a time that person's death might have been. Though because this cemetery, or whatever it is, is so new, it couldn't have been more than seven years ago."

"It was only last year—this week's his anniversary. And he was all right as a person, not great—I don't want to lie to you. But thanks." He patted the man's back and got into his car. He backed up, pulled away and saw in the rearview mirror the man waving at him.

Takes

Man's waiting in the service elevator right next to the passenger elevator. Someone comes—a woman, hopes it's a young one, through the front door or from one of the apartments upstairs or on this floor—he'll step out behind her with the knife, threaten her with it, take her in the automatic elevator rather than this hand-operated one to the top floor, walk her up to the roof, knife always on her throat, he always behind her and threatening softly but with a real scary tone in his voice "One scream and I'll use it; make even a move from this knife or to see me and I'll kill you," take her to a good dark out-of-the-way spot on the roof—all depending what lights from the other buildings' windows are on it—and rape her. She'll never see his face and his voice won't be his own. She doesn't put up a fuss, he'll leave her there gagged and tied up. He's scouted out the building. Not many tenants come in or leave their apartments this late, but it's worth the wait. Someone will come. Lots of single women in this neighborhood, so has to be a few in this building too. But on Saturday night, most, he bets, will be with men friends. One won't though and that's who.

Tenant on the eighth floor. Can't sleep. Something's up. Hasn't always been right when she thought something bad was going to happen, but enough times she has. It's not from any crazy imagination she's thinking this. The winos were really loud tonight. Few more bottles and things smashed on the street or whatever they're smashed against than usual too. And a couple more souped-up cars and motorcycles than she's used to racing past her building too. Why don't the police do something? If it's because they don't know of these things going on or they're too lazy to patrol or can't because of cutbacks, then why don't people call them more? This city. She turns the TV off. Get some sleep.

Young woman's mother in Connecticut. Thinking about her daughter. She went to New York to do graduate work in painting. Took an apartment with another young woman, a friend from college. But the building's bad. Filthy, poorly maintained, bell system that doesn't work; a firetrap, she's sure. Even if some of the neighborhood's okay, and some of the river buildings even elegant, and as co-ops or rented apartments, quite expensive, much of it's very bad. Welfare hotels. Cheap rooming houses. Awful-looking men and women on the street day and night. Little park nearby where men drink and some dope and urinate in the open and make vulgar remarks to passing women and all sorts of other things. Beggars. In the *Times* she's read of break-ins and muggings and seen a city crime statistic chart that put her neighborhood near the top. Worried.

Man in a cab going acrosstown. Should have got out of the cab and escorted her upstairs. Didn't like the looks of her building and block. But then he hardly knows her. She might have thought he was being funny in a way—forward, not funny. And he had this cab, was in it, did only promise to take her to the street door, or rather: just see, while he sat in the cab, she got inside that door, and then he might not have got another cab after he left her building or not so fast. Could have asked the cab to wait while he saw her to her apartment door. Now he thinks of it. But she said she'd be all right. He did ask. And he's sure that no matter how hard he insisted on taking her to her apartment door, she would have said no. *Still*.

Woman's in the lobby, presses the elevator button. Light above the elevator door says the car's on the top floor, the eighth. Slow elevator, takes days to get down. She doesn't like waiting in this creepy lobby. Anyway, her friend Phoebe will be upstairs and they can talk about tonight. The man she met. He was nice. Took her home in a cab, wouldn't let her share the fare with him. She wishes she had accepted his suggestion and let him walk her to her door. But then she would have had to invite him in. And offer him a coffee or a beer, when really all she wants to do, if Phoebe's up—she'll be up—is talk a little with her and go to sleep. Elevator's about here. It's here.

Man thinks now's the time. She's a good-looking one. Long legs, big ass. She'll screw well. He'll screw her well. He'll screw her till she cries for more, more. He steps out. She turns around. Knife's out. Damn, she saw him. "Don't say a word or I'll kill you right here." He gets behind her and puts the knife to her neck. Opens the elevator door, knife always against her neck. "We're going to the roof. I know this building. Don't say a word, make a peep—nothing—don't even sneak a look at me again or you're dead. I know how to get out of this building easily so I'll be out of here before you hit the ground. Now get in."

She gets in. She doesn't believe this. What should she do? This is a dream. A nightmare. It's the worst thing that's ever happened to her. Think, think. That knife. It pricks. They go up. He pressed eight. He said "roof." Maybe someone will stop the elevator on the fourth floor, fifth. There's only one outside button for each floor. No down and up buttons—just one, and if you press that button when you want to do down and the elevator's going up, it stops. Please. Someone.

It's too late to call her, her mother thinks. She'd like to. She wants very much to speak to Corinne, tell her how worried she is about her. Tell her that Dad and she will give her a hundred dollars a month extra to find a better building to live in. Two hundred. It'll be a sacrifice for them, but it just shows how anxious they are about where she's living now. If she's going to live in that city, she'll tell her, then it has to be on these terms. Of course she could say no, she likes where she's living now, took months to find and then paint and set up, doesn't want to take any more money from them than she already is and so on, and they really wouldn't be able to do anything about it. It's too late to call. But it's Saturday. She dials. Corinne's phone rings. If she answers it, or if Phoebe answers it—she hasn't once thought of Phoebe, for instance how she'd take to Corinne's parents subsidizing most of their rent—she'll apologize for calling this late, but both will have to know she only has their best interests at heart. That's not enough. She slams down the receiver. She can wait till tomorrow? Has to, since Corinne will see her anxiety at this hour as bordering on mania. Just another nine or ten hours. Eleven's okay to call on Sundays for women that age. Even if they're with men friends who stayed the night, which, let's face it, could well be the case. She goes upstairs to wash up for bed. Her husband says from the bedroom "What've you been doing? I heard you slamming the phone down, picking it up, then slamming it again." "I only slammed it once. I was worried about Corinne. Worked it out in my head though, so it's now all okay."

Roommate at a party downtown. Wonders if Corinne's home by now. She's sure she's expecting her to be there when she gets home. Note she left will explain it or should. Something like "Aaron called. Sudden invite to big bash at a south of Soho artist's loft and wanted me to join him. I know. Swore I'd grind away at the books all weekend and maybe never see Aaron again, but what, dear, can I say?" They have a phone here? If so, she'll call Corinne and say she doubts she'll be coming home tonight, and she should try to do that before two. She's just about never seen or heard Corinne up after two. "Excuse me," to a woman she thinks is one of the three people giving the party, "but is there by any chance a phone in this place I may use?" "As long as it's not to out of town," the woman says. "Positively not." "Actually, if you're a good friend of either of the other hosts, you can make that call to as far west as Columbus, south as Washington, and as far north as Boston, let's say."

She's also a very pleasant girl, man in the cab thinks. Attractive. Even pretty. He'd definitely call her pretty, even beautiful in some ways, though he doubts a couple of his friends would. Still. And she had spark. Bright, besides. Far as he could make out, bright as any woman he's met in a year. He's definitely phoning her tomorrow. Monday night, not tomorrow. Doesn't want to appear too eager. Why not? She seemed like she'd like eagerness. Directed at her, but not just to score. She complained how most men she meets these days don't really care or get excited about anything but making money and getting ahead. Don't really read, don't think much about serious things, aren't interested in much art other than movies and music. She didn't say he was different than they but implied he was. She also gave him her phone number willingly enough. He likes her name. She seems to come from a good family: intelligent, moral, involved, well-off. He thinks she sort of took to him too. Maybe that's why he should act fast: so she doesn't forget why she was attracted to him, if she was. Tomorrow night. No, Monday's soon enough. He hopes she paints well. If she doesn't, he could always say at first—later he could level with her more—"Hell, what do I know?"

Top floor. Roof stairs and door. Always trying to get a look at him to see if he means it—seemed he did. Had one of the most maniacal faces she's even seen, when she saw him just that one glimpse. Slim, young, smelly, wiry, ruthless, cagey-looking. He's crazy. He's going to kill her. If it was just robbery he would have taken the bag from her downstairs and fled. Knife isn't on her neck anymore. Rape and possibly kill her. She has to find a way to get away. She has to scream, run, kick, maybe on the roof. Now she's thinking. Roof, where there's space. Stairs he's got her trapped. This building's attached to the corner one and unless there's barbed wire or something separating the two roofs, she can make a run for it yelling all the time. Pick up a brick if they have one on the roof and he's cornered her against something like a wall or by a roof edge and throw it at him. Anything: teeth, knees and fists and then down a fire escape, but to escape. There's one that goes all the way past her bedroom window to the narrow alleyway on the ground floor. Corner building must have one too. If not, down her building's fire escape screaming, knocking, banging, breaking all the windows along the way if she has to till someone comes, wakes up, shouts, whatever, but helps chase the man away.

Tenant hears footsteps on the roof right above her. Who could be up there this hour? Trouble. Either some junkies got in the building or corner one next door and got to the roof that way and are shooting up. Or winos or runaways or just plain bums making a home for the night up there? Why can't it rain now or snow? Get them off. She just hopes the roof door's locked tight so they don't start walking down the building's stairs and making noise and throwing up in the hallways as what happened a couple of times or trying all the doors. What else could it be up there but something awful? She hopes not someone forced to go for the worst of purposes. That's happened on one or two other buildings around here but never hers.

"Now you know what I want," the man says. "I want to screw you but I want it without holding the knife to your face. That way it'll be better for me and easier and quicker for you. Then if you're good to me and a good little girl all around and give no trouble I'll let you go. You're a real piece of ass, you know? I could tell right away you screw well and that you've screwed around a lot. You got the face for it. Saucy. Sexy. So, you going to do it like I say? You don't, you're dead."

"No, I don't want to do it with you," the woman says. And then louder: "Now let me alone. Let me get by you and downstairs. Now please—I'm asking—please!" He stabs her in the chest. She raises her arms. He stabs her several times. She goes down. She screams. She says "Help, I'm being murdered." He gets on one knee and stabs her where he thinks her heart is.

"Stop that, stop that," the tenant shouts out her window. "Whoever it is, leave that girl alone. Help, police, someone's killing someone upstairs. On the roof. Stop that, you butcher, stop that, stop."

"Help me, I'm dying," the woman says. "Stupid bitch," the man says. He jumps up. Lights have gone on in some of the apartment windows in buildings that overlook the roof. "Shit," he says. "Hey you there," a man says from one window. "What is it, what's going on?" a man says from a window right next to that one. "I've called the police," a woman shouts from what seems like the building he's on. "They're coming. They're on their way. Everybody call to make sure they come. Girl, don't be afraid. They're coming. People from this building will be up there for you too." "Shit," he says and leaps over the low wall to get to the next building's fire escape.

Her mother thinks about the dream she just had. All the apartment buildings around hers were falling down, one after the other. She lives in a suburban townhouse and has never lived in anything but a private home, but in the dream she was in she lived in an apartment in a tall old apartment building in a large city that looked more European than American. The buildings collapsed straight down as if heavy explosives had been set off under them. For a while it seemed the window was a TV screen and she was watching the buildings fall in slow motion in a documentary. She was with her three daughters, all about four to eight years younger than they are now, and her husband

and mother, who's dead. Then her building was falling. She held out her arms to her family and said "Here, come into me." Her arms became progressively longer as each person came into her. She kissed their heads in a row—they were all as small as little children now—and started crying. Then they were at her family's gravesite behind her grandparents' farmhouse, burying her mother. "This proves life can go on," she said to her husband, daughters and grandmother. She doesn't know what the last part of the dream means. There is no farmhouse or family gravesite. Her parents and grandparents are buried in three different enormous cemeteries. Where was her son in the dream? She gets out of bed, goes to the kitchen, writes down the dream and what she thinks the end of it means. "That everything will be OK with C (living in her city hovel)? That I really needn't be anxious about any of my kids or really about anything in life (how'd I come to that last conclusion?)? That if people stay in mind & memory (just about the same thing; I realize that) they're never really dead? That living, dying, illness, fraility, tragedy, mayhem, mishaps, madness, revolutions, terrorism (from inside & out) and the rest of it are all quite normal? (Was that all you were going to say?) That we're all basically entwined &—now stop all that; it was never in it. Then what? Time for God? Not at any price & why'd that idea pop in? (To interpret it theologically, that's all.) An important dream though, start to end, no matter what I don't make of it. Read all this back tomorrow. Underscore that: read, read! Maybe then."

Her father can't sleep. He feels for his wife in bed. She left it before but is there now. "Hilda, you up? I can't sleep; want to talk." No answer or movement. Why'd she have to worry him so? Not that he can't handle it, but— He gets up, goes to the bathroom, drinks a glass of water. That was stupid. Meant to take two aspirins first. He gets the aspirins out of the medicine cabinet, puts them in his mouth and washes them down with another glass of water. Now he'll feel better. In about fifteen minutes. And his dreams are usually more vivid and peaceful in theme when he takes aspirins. His doctor thinks he should take an aspirin every other night to reduce the fat or plaque on his blood vessel walls. He doesn't mind, especially for the side benefits of a more peaceful sleep and dreams, but usually forgets to.

The woman's being treated by paramedics. She gives a description of her attacker and details of what happened. "Honestly, try not to talk," one of the paramedics says. "Yes, you probably shouldn't," a policeman says. She says "No, I want you to know what happened. If I go over it enough times, you'll get everything. I came into the building. We're still on my building?" "Yes, of course," the policeman says. "I meant, he didn't drag me over the parapet to the next building?" "If he did, he brought you back or you got back here on your own." "No, what am I talking of?" she says. "I came into the building. I'll proceed chronologically, no digressions. I came into the building." "I really don't want her talking," the paramedic says. "You heard him, Miss. Don't talk." "I came into the building. He was waiting for me in the service elevator. That elevator ought to be locked at night, not left open. People can hide there. I'm digressing, but so what? The lobby door should have a better lock. Anyone, with a little force, can push the door open when it's locked. The building should have better lights. Look at the lights when you leave in the lobby and hallways. Thirty watts, maybe. One to a hallway if you're lucky. There's a city law. My roommate's checked. She's studying to be a lawyer. Where is she?" "If you mean Miss Kantor," the policeman says, "she's not home. We've been inside your apartment. To look for your attacker. I hope you don't mind." "There's a city law saying the wattage should be higher, Phoebe said. Minimum of two lights too. In case one goes out. He had a long knife. Said he'd kill me unless. Well, he nearly did. Maybe he will have. No he won't. I should say that. No he won't." "You shouldn't

say anything," the paramedic says. "This officer and I say *don't*."
"But I wouldn't have sex with him. Why would I? It would
have been worse than anything. He was filthy. A beast. A jungle.
I thought I could escape on the roof. I should have tried to
break away sooner. In the lobby. That way I would have had a
chance. But I was so scared. I couldn't think. I got my wits
about me going up the elevator. His knife seemed shined. Maybe
he shines it with polish. He was sick enough. Maybe I should
have let him do it. Screw me, he said. Maybe it would have
been worth it, filth and all. When you can't do anything." "Now
that's enough. Absolutely no more talk." "This has all been
very valuable, Corinne," the policeman says, "but this man is
right. Save your strength. I insist. For your own sake." "All
right."

He's in a bar about ten blocks away having a beer and scotch.
He got about twenty dollars from her bag. He's standing a man
he just met to a drink. He says "Oh boy, did I have a good
one tonight. Met a chickie on Broadway. She hadn't been laid
for months. She just looked at me and said 'I'll give you a
twenty if you lay me in a basement I know of—it's the only
place we can go. If you don't want to, just say so and I won't
say another word about it.' No bullshit. Under a bus shelter.
We were both waiting for the number four and she turns to me
and says this. 'My husband's home,' she says. 'He never lays
me. He likes men only now. You don't like men,' she says, 'do
you? I hope not.' That's what she said. I told her I like women
only. All parts of them, not just the ones that count. And I can
do it all night. This is what I tell her. 'Or at least I used to.
Now only half the night which is fine for most ladies, okay?' So
we went to this basement. I was so hot by now I could have
done it to her right on the street. She gave me the twenty. It
was cozy down there. Even had a mattress and nice little table
lamp on the floor. She took me into an alleyway and made me
shut my eyes the last minute of walking so I wouldn't ever find

the place alone. Even turned me all the way around a few times so I'd be all mixed up in my directions. I bet she did it with lots of guys down there. But twenty. For laying her. She was great. Clean. Wet. Smelled good. A Mother Earth, no Miss Twiggy. Big hips. Big tits. Big everything. I felt I was swimming in her. I would've paid her if I had a twenty and she asked. If I'd known how good she was, is what I meant, for I don't pay anyone for sex. Things are free now, free now, you don't have to pay. Women walking around without panties and bras, kids doing it before your eyes in cars—man, it's all over the place. But to get paid for it? Hey, I'll take it! But that was it. Twice. That was all she could take, and to lay it on the line to you, me too. She was too much. She nearly killed me. Then we got dressed and left together and she made me shut my eyes again till we got into the street. She never gave me her name or phone number or address, but I bet she lives in that same building but higher up. You think she had a husband?" Other man raises his shoulders. "I don't. I think that's just her line so you don't think of going to her apartment right after to rob her. You know, some guys could just get her address from her bag while they're even balling her. 'If we meet, we meet,' she said when I said what about us doing this again sometime? 'You were the best,' was the last thing she said to me. Even if I wasn't, what do I care? All I know is she gave me a great time and made me twenty bills heavier."

The other man says "That's a fantastic story—unbeatable— I only wish it was me," and thinks if ever a guy was full of it, this one's it. He downs his drink, says "Got enough for a refill?—I'm a little low." "I think I can make it." "Thanks. I'm going to hit the pisser. Tell Rich for me to put a soda in back of mine this time," and goes to the men's room.

Her parents' phone rings. He looks at the clock. "Who can be calling so late? Probably a wrong number. You answer it, please, or just let it ring. I can't even move off the bed." Which one of her children? she thinks, going to the phone. It can't be anything but bad. It's rung too many times.

Her sister's sitting in a movie theater in Seattle. The phone's ringing in her apartment. Another sister's working in the sun on an archaeological dig in Egypt. This work is harder than she ever thought it would be, she thinks, and no fun. She wishes she was back home. Face it: she's homesick. She never would have believed it but she is. Her brother's sleeping in his college fraternity house. The person calling the house gets a recorded message that the phone's been temporarily disconnected.

The tenant leaves the building very early, says good morning to the policeman guarding the front door, asks how the girl is. "I haven't heard." "Do you know if they caught the man who did it yet?" "I don't think so." She goes to church, kneels, prays for the girl's life and that the man is caught and that the whole city becomes more peaceful again, at least as peaceful as it was about twenty years ago, but if only one prayer's answered then that the girl lives. She sits, covers her eyes with her hands, just let things come into her. It's quiet in here, she thinks. For now, this is the only place.

The man who took her home the night before gets up around nine, has coffee, goes out for the *Times* and a quart of milk and two bagels, dumps half the newspaper sections into a trash can, reads the front page of the news section as he walks home, reads the sports and book sections while having a toasted bagel and coffee at home, looks at his watch, 9:42, still much too early, slips in a tape cassette, does warm-up exercises, goes out for a six-mile or one-hour run, whichever comes first, comes back, did good time—must have been all the alcohol last night that gave him so much sugar—showers, shaves, checks the time, 11:38, no, not yet; twelve, on Sunday, is really the earliest he can call someone he just met. If she worked as hard as she said she did this week—studying, painting, her waitress job every other week-day afternoon and all-day Saturday—she'll need a good ten-hour sleep. Once she gets up she'll probably need an hour just to get started. One. Call her at one.

ACB0559   11/6/90

PS
3554
I92
L68
1989

0 00 02 0498040 3
MIDDLEBURY COLLEGE